Lexie

Lexie

by Audrey Couloumbis

illustrated by Julia Denos

A Yearling Book

Text copyright © 2011 by Audrey Couloumbis
Cover art and interior illustrations copyright © 2011 by Julia Denos

All rights reserved. Published in the United States by Yearling,
an imprint of Random House Children's Books, a division of
Random House, Inc., New York. Originally published in hardcover in
the United States by Random House Children's Books, New York, in 2011.

Yearling and the jumping horse design are registered
trademarks of Random House, Inc.

Visit us on the Web! randomhouse.com/kids

Educators and librarians, for a variety of teaching tools, visit us at
randomhouse.com/teachers

The Library of Congress has cataloged the hardcover
edition of this work as follows:
Couloumbis, Audrey.
Lexie / Audrey Couloumbis. — 1st ed.
p. cm.
Summary: When ten-year-old Lexie goes with her father to the beach
for a week, she is surprised to find that he has invited his girlfriend and
her two sons to join them for the entire week.
ISBN 978-0-375-85632-7 (trade) — ISBN 978-0-375-95632-4 (lib. bdg.)
ISBN 978-0-375-85633-4 (pbk.) — ISBN 978-0-375-89322-3 (ebook)
[1. Fathers and daughters—Fiction. 2. Divorce—Fiction.
3. Remarriage—Fiction. 4. Beaches—Fiction. 5. Vacations—Fiction.]
I. Title.
PZ7.C8305Le 2011
[Fic]—dc22   2010020751

Printed in the United States of America

10 9 8 7 6 5 4 3 2 1

First Yearling Edition 2012

For Hannah,
who likes cold eggs

Lexie ⭑

One

I should have been on my way to the shore. So of course I was sitting on the window seat, reading.

"Lexie, your dad will be here any minute," Mom said, coming into my room like she was on her way to a fire. "You aren't packed."

My shorts and tops were folded and stacked on my bed. Sweatshirts and jeans too, because it gets cold at night at the Jersey shore. I was supposed to put them in my suitcase. Mom had been bagging stuff to make lunch at the shore. It was almost time to eat already.

I didn't shut my book. I said, "Daddy's late."

"He should have been here over an hour ago. Almost two hours ago. Did I rush you then?"

"No."

"Right, because we knew he would be late. Now he's very late, which means he'll be here any minute." Mom got my old pink and white polka-dotted suitcase off the high shelf in my closet. Babyish, maybe, but I still liked it. "Let's get this stuff packed up."

I closed my book. "It's going to be weird without you there."

"It's going to be weird without you here," Mom said. She was using the voice of *If people can climb mountains, we can do this.* "But we'll manage."

In about one minute, she packed everything. I got up to go over and lie on my bed. "The thing is," I said, "I don't want to go."

"You love the shore," Mom said. "You love your dad. You're going to have a fine time and you're going to forget to call me every day."

"I won't," I said, and started to feel exactly the way I didn't want to feel. Like I might cry. I stared hard at the ceiling. "I won't forget."

Mom said, "Just don't call while my favorite shows are on, okay?"

"That's ridiculous," I said. "You don't watch TV."

"I'm probably going to start." Mom sat down on the edge of my bed. She looked like she might cry too.

"It's just for this week," I reminded her. "Then it's only on the weekends."

"Right." Mom stretched out next to me and put her head on my pillow so both of us were looking at the ceiling.

"I brought a few of my favorite beach books home last year," I said. "I can leave them with you."

"Leave one for me," Mom said. *Beachcombing. Or Out of the Ocean.*"

"I could leave you *Babymouse.*"

"No, no, you're right in the middle of it," Mom said and I was so glad.

But I felt bad too. "It isn't fair that you can't come to the shore."

"Your dad can't live here anymore, I can't stay there anymore." Her eyes had closed and her voice sounded like she might fall asleep. "That's the way things get worked out with divorce."

"I don't like it."

"I'm sorry about that, I really am." She got up and started going through my closet. "A big part of growing up is dealing with things we don't like."

She pulled out two dresses for me.

"Daddy won't take me anywhere I need a dress." Mom put one of the dresses back in the closet. I asked, "How come Daddy's late and *we're* hurrying?"

"I don't like to keep him waiting back, that's why," Mom said.

"What are you going to do while I'm gone?" I asked her.

"George said he'll pick me up at work and take me to breakfast every morning."

"Every morning?" George had been her boyfriend for about a month now. He was always on time, and Mom liked that.

"Pancakes, omelettes, waffles, scrambled, french toast," she said. "Something different each day."

"George always keeps his promises," I said. I

didn't think it was always important to be on time. But promises mattered.

"He's a good guy," Mom said. We were quiet for a few seconds and then she said, "Lexie, your dad loves you as much as I do. He's just got a looser style."

"I know that."

We heard the car horn. Daddy bought one of those oooh-gah horns right after they got the divorce. He said he got it so I would know it was him. I looked out the window and saw our car and suddenly I wanted to go. I already missed Mom, and I still wanted to go.

"I'll call you," I said.

"I didn't check your knapsack," Mom said as I unzipped it. "Toothbrush, hair comb?"

"And my bathing suit." I stuffed the book I was reading inside. I left the others for Mom.

"Did you put in the sunscreen?"

"Daddy always forgets to tell me to put it on."

"You're old enough to remember. You're practically preadolescent."

"Don't rush me."

Two

Driving to the shore, Daddy kept telling me riddles. "What's green and sings 'It's a Small World' when you plug it in?"

"I don't know," I said.

"Electric lettuce."

"Silly." He makes these up himself.

He said, "What's yellow, runs downhill, and makes everybody else run and hide?"

"Don't have a clue."

"Baby diarrhea."

"Gross." Really.

He said, "What spits, throws sparks, and can climb a tree at the speed of light?"

"I'm afraid to ask."

"A cat on Rollerblades."

"Weird." But I laughed. I like his riddles.

He said, "Why did the ballerina wear a tutu?"

"To keep her tush-tush warm?"

Daddy looked over at me. "Very cute," he said. "We could come up with a riddle for that."

"So what's the answer really?"

"Because the one-one was too little and the three-three was too big."

I didn't feel like making up riddles. I said, "Can't we listen to the radio?"

Between the songs we sang along with, we made plans to build the biggest sand castle ever and eat hamburgers every day. Except today, when we were having turkey sandwiches.

We didn't stop for lunch. We ate a bag of chips and drank soda so we'd get to the shore faster. Even if I didn't know the way, I would know when we nearly get there. When you open the car windows, the air sort of sticks to your skin. It smells like tuna fish out there. For some reason, no one minds.

I sat up straighter so I'd see the water first.

"I want to find a hermit crab this year," I said. "I already bought a fish tank and put gravel in the bottom."

"Cool," Daddy said.

"Mom helped me plant some parsley in the tank and we put in a few grass seeds, because maybe a hermit crab would like that."

"Sure, who doesn't want a lawn?"

"I'm serious," I said. "We also saved a blue plastic lid. We'll put water in it for a hermit crab pool."

"Okay, well, maybe we'll find one," he said. "If not, we can probably buy one. Doesn't one of those shops on the boardwalk sell them? They have decals of flags and flowers on the shells."

"I'd rather find my own."

Daddy said, "I asked somebody to come out to the shore for a visit." There was something in his voice, like when he tells me he got me something special for Christmas and lets me wonder what it is.

I didn't ask who was coming to the shore. I looked at his face, still half smiling, and at the way his hair falls over his forehead. I looked away.

Last week I'd heard Mom tell a friend of hers that she used to love the way Daddy looks. Then she said she would never marry another man who didn't comb his hair back off his face.

"I thought you might like some company," Daddy said.

I turned the radio off. "I thought we were each other's company."

"It'll be fun to have Vicky out here," he said. "Besides, it's a nice thing to do for friends. Get them out of the city heat."

Mom was still in Baltimore in the sweltering heat—that's what she called it when sweat ran down our sides in lines. This would be our first time here without her.

"It'll be fun to have Vicky out here," he said again.

I turned on the radio and we didn't talk anymore until we got to Seaville.

"I can see the water," Daddy said, like I should be getting excited.

I could see the water too, and across it, I could see the trees on the long barrier island where our house stood. Technically, this water was the ocean. What Mom and I do is look out across the water to where it meets the sky. We weren't quite there yet.

"Close, but no cigar," I said, because that was what George says when something is almost right but not exactly. I'm not sure what cigars have to do with it.

We passed Bongo Billy's ice cream stand, the one with plastic palm trees and a monkey with eyes that do a slow blink. A long line of people already stood waiting for cones.

"Nearly there," Daddy said. He sounded excited about it.

I sat forward, watching for the bridge.

"You met Vicky, remember?" he said. "You liked her."

I met Vicky in Daddy's hardware store. She'd brought in her broken vacuum cleaner, dragging it through the snow, asking if someone could tell her how to fix it. Daddy fixed it.

A few weeks later we ran into her in the grocery store. She and Daddy talked like friends and I thought it was because of the vacuum cleaner. Then Vicky said how much she liked the movie they'd seen and I knew it wasn't just the vacuum cleaner.

Maybe I said she seemed nice. I never said I liked her.

I didn't care if he wanted Vicky to come out sometime. On one of our weekends. For a whole day. This was supposed to be our week at the shore, Daddy's and mine.

We turned onto the bridge that leads to our road. For a long time, I didn't know this was a bridge. I thought it was a road with water on both sides.

A lady in loose pants waved to us when we stopped at the other side. I didn't wave back. "Who's that?" I asked. The breeze made her pants ripple like a skirt. People always wear stuff like that around the shore. When they aren't wearing bathing suits, anyway.

"I don't know," Daddy said. "Someone friendly. You heard me, right? Vicky is coming out here."

Another time when I saw Daddy—the snow was gone then so it was around Easter—I found a scarf in the car and Daddy said, *Vicky's*. And I said, *The movies?* And he said, *No, she had a problem with her car and I gave her a ride home.*

That didn't sound like a date to me. I figured she must have been going to the movies with somebody else by now. I didn't expect her to show up at the shore. "You gave old Mrs. Steadman a ride home once," I said. "You didn't ask her out to the shore."

"Give me a break here, would you?" Daddy said. We were on the last turn before our road. I looked out at the water.

"What day?" I asked, hoping we could get Vicky's visit over with quick. Like being the first one in at the doctor's office. It's much worse to wait around and see little kids come out with tears on their faces and lollipops in their mouths.

If Vicky came early, tomorrow or the next day, we could settle down to enjoy ourselves sooner.

Daddy cleared his throat, the way he does when he talks with Mom and she's getting mad. He looked a little sunburned. It wasn't sunburn, I knew that. The sunburned look comes right after he clears his throat if Mom is going to be very unhappy.

For some reason I couldn't explain, I almost cried. I sucked it in, though. Daddy hates it when I cry.

"They're going to be with us all week," Daddy said. "She's bringing her kids."

"Her kids?"

"They're about your age."

"You could have told me." I could hardly breathe. "I thought this vacation was for us."

"It is, honey," Daddy said. He was using that same voice, *I can see the water.* "We're going to have lots of fun."

I felt like I'd been tricked. "Does Mom know?" He didn't answer. He frowned, which meant Mom didn't know either.

Three

We turned into our parking spot, the gravel making popping sounds under the tires. There were cars parked in other spots already. Gravel is to keep the wheels from getting stuck in the sand. We sat for a moment, the way we always do, taking everything in.

The houses are on tall stilts to hold them above the water during high tide. Windows had been propped open with sticks to let fresh air into the houses. Quilts flapped from the deck railings.

Standing on the deck is like being up in a tree house without the leafy branches all around.

Like being on a ship headed out to sea. You get a brave feeling, because before you get used to it, it's scary.

A couple of dogs chased each other below, sand flying out behind them. From the car, we could look straight under the houses to where the ocean meets the sky.

Everything looked the way it should.

And I still didn't feel like I was all the way there yet. Lately I would get this feeling of falling behind and not being able to catch up. It's the feeling of being divorced, I think. I stared out at the water and waited for the feeling to go away.

Nothing protects the houses from strong winds, so the first thing we say is "Well, it's still here," like, boy, are we amazed.

"Well, it's still here," Daddy said, and things felt almost normal again.

Our house is a silvery gray because that's the color wood turns by the sea. Some of the houses are painted bright colors in the spring, and by the next year, the sides that face the sea are going gray again.

We took stuff out of the car and climbed the

steps to the porch. It's the porch on this side because it's screened in. On the ocean side it's open and we call it the deck.

The wind was blowing sand over the porch boards. I could hardly wait to take off my sneakers and walk barefoot in wet sand. First I had to help carry stuff.

Inside, the house smelled the by-the-ocean smell that makes Mom sneeze and open all the windows. It had that too-quiet sound of coming in for the first time of the summer.

Daddy looked around like he didn't know for sure what to do. He was loaded down with a knapsack and two duffel bags and a grocery bag from an expensive store where Mom never shops. He let everything drop to the floor right inside the door.

I carried the bag full of lunch meat and the other stuff Mom packed for us to the long room that opens out onto the deck. This room is part bookcase, part dining room, part kitchen, and part laundry and utility room. The *utility* part means the water heater is there behind the washing machine.

I put the bag I was carrying on the table, thinking about how hungry I was. But Daddy went straight outside, so I did too.

We stood at the edge of the deck and let the wind blow our hair every which way. The railing is there so nobody falls off, but that brave shivery feeling still happens for a minute.

This was when Mom usually took over. Daddy and I always headed straight out to splash around a little.

"Let's check out the water," Daddy said.

I kicked off my sneakers and we ran down the wooden steps. Daddy started doing these fast runs across the waves on the shore, something he calls wind sprints. Water splashed all around him.

I stood on the wet sand and waited for the water to come. It rushed over the beach in a curved line, barely touching me, leaving sea foam bubbling between my toes. Sand trickled away, trailing the water.

Further down the shore were some small birds, running toward the ocean as it washed out, and running away as it washed back in.

Daddy ran past, splashing water as his feet

slapped down, and I laughed when some cold drops hit me. And finally the water swept in, foamy as soapsuds, covering my feet.

I ran with Daddy a couple of times. He's still too fast for me.

"Hungry?" he asked me as he came to a stop, breathing hard.

"I was hungry before."

"Race you!" Daddy shot across the sand and up the stairs. I couldn't keep up. "One of these times," I shouted as I ran after him. Mom always said that when I lost a race.

I unpacked enough stuff to make turkey sandwiches while Daddy checked the water pipes. My stomach growled the whole time. When Daddy unscrewed the mayonnaise jar for me, he said, "Oh, mayo. I forgot about that."

"Well, Mom sent enough."

"No, I mean, I forgot about mayonnaise entirely. I don't think I've eaten it since last summer."

He forgets all kinds of things. "Do you want a little or a lot?" I asked him.

"I love mayo," he said. "Slather it on." He went outside to do something to get the water heater working. To turn on the water, I remembered, as air and water began to blast from the kitchen faucet.

I turned it off there and in the bathroom. Now that there was water in the pipes, the house sounded right. Not noisy, once I'd turned the water off, but not silent either.

Daddy came back into the kitchen, carrying his grocery bag and some sheets he'd scooped up on his way in. "Put everything in the fridge," he said, putting his grocery bag on the top shelf.

The refrigerator hadn't been turned on yet, and the doors stood open. Inside it, a brown smear of ketchup or something was growing fuzzy white mold.

Usually when Mom closed the house at the end of summer, she wiped out the refrigerator so it would be clean, clean, clean when we came back. Last year we'd left early. We left Daddy there by himself, and he didn't know how to clean up, not really.

There were crumbs in the bottom of the fridge and a yellowed piece of waxed paper that had been folded around a sandwich last summer. Over the winter, mice had chewed through the paper. Maybe Daddy left the sandwich there by accident.

He shoved the sheets into the washing machine. He bumped the refrigerator door shut when he went past again.

"You have to turn it on," I said.

"What?"

"The refrigerator. You have to turn it on. There's a dial, remember?"

"Oh, yeah." He opened the door and turned the dial. "I have to go back out. I forgot to turn on the gas."

I thought about the table. Mom had always pushed it up against the kitchen counter. That left three sides for sitting at, which was perfect for three people.

I pushed and pulled the table over to the sliding doors and put one chair at each end. That way, when we came in for breakfast in the morning it would seem like that was how things had always been. Sort of.

A cabbagey smell invaded the kitchen. It was the smell of the gas coming on. I looked through the drawers for the matches, because that was what Mom always did when we smelled the gas.

I remembered Vicky was coming, probably tomorrow. I figured she wouldn't show up before breakfast. Maybe she was a person who slept late on weekends. We'd have most of the day to ourselves.

Daddy came in and used the matches to light the stove. Then he stretched out on the floor, poking lit matches inside the water heater until he got it started. It took a lot more tries than the stove. By then, I had our sandwiches ready.

The deck chairs were still inside, in a tiny bedroom we use like a closet. So we sat on the deck, letting our legs hang over while we ate. Our elbows rested on the lower railing. My legs felt a little itchy where sand had dried on my skin.

The tide was coming in and water would cover the bottom step. Lap, slap. It was quiet at the shore, except for the sound of the ocean. That went on all day and all night, lap, slap. The ocean seemed quiet. But it drowned out all the other noise around us.

We couldn't hear the neighbor's radio or cars on the road. If we didn't look to the left or the right, if we looked straight out to sea, we could imagine we were the last people on earth.

24

Daddy asked, "Wouldn't it be great to live here all year around?" which was the next thing we said every year.

I tried to remember what Mom used to say.

Voices came from inside the house. Daddy's face brightened. "They're early," he said.

Four

Daddy stood up and set his sandwich on the deck railing, so I did too. He'd only had about two bites, and my sandwich wasn't half eaten either.

They came outside one by one. First a little boy running, his arms out before him as if he was driving a runaway truck. He made noises like a truck. *Vrrrroom! Vrmmmmm.* He braked to a stop. *Eeeeeeeech!*

Then Vicky, looking happy and excited. She was wearing all white clothes, a long skirt and a sheer scarf that hung to her knees and lifted in the breeze like she was in a commercial. "We would have knocked but the door was open."

"That's the welcome sign," Daddy said in a big voice.

"Then it's okay that we're here a couple of hours early?" she asked. "I couldn't hold the team down any longer," she said with a helpless shrug. "I figured you'd had all afternoon to get things set up."

"We got here a little later than I expected," Daddy said.

The little boy *vrrrroom*ed once and sort of bucked, like his motor was about to run through a stoplight. He throttled down to a dull humming sound, his hands resting on an imaginary steering wheel.

His hands were dirty. Not mud-puddle dirty. More like he'd reached under the bed for something and picked up a lot of lint. I thought maybe he'd eaten something sticky in the car.

"We need to wash our hands," Vicky said, although she didn't seem to be saying it to anyone. So it wasn't too surprising that Daddy didn't move to show her where the bathroom was.

Daddy looked like he didn't know what to do with his arms. He kept crossing them and un-crossing them. Finally, he leaned back on the deck railing like somebody who didn't know where the bathroom was.

An older boy—older than me, anyway—sort of slouched into the doorway behind Vicky, look-ing bored. He had a knapsack slung over one shoulder and wore earphones that he didn't take off to talk to Daddy. "Hey, dude."

"Ben," Daddy said.

I didn't know they knew each other. I could see how they probably would. "You never answer when people call you dude," I reminded Daddy.

"This is Lexie," Daddy said.

"Cool," the kid said. He'd pulled his hair back into a very short ponytail. More like a tuft. And the hair at the sides had pulled loose and hung like parentheses over his earphones. "Some view from here," he said.

"This is Ben," Vicky told me, "and Harris. Stop that and say hello to Lexie."

"*Vrrrroom!*" Harris took off around the deck.

Ben spoke up. "I'm fourteen, and Harris

is three. He likes you to call him Mack."

I looked doubtfully at Harris. "Mack?"

"As in Mack truck."

Harris rumbled once more around the deck before he ran back into the house. Vicky sighed, looking pretty much the way she'd looked standing over the vacuum cleaner. She reminded me of somebody.

There's this old TV show that Mom loves, *The Mary Tyler Moore Show*, on one of the cable stations. That was who Vicky acted like. Mary. She looked like Mary, a little bit. When I got a voice like Mary's, or Vicky's, Mom always said, *Don't whine.*

"Where's the girl?" I asked.

"What girl?" Ben asked, and I was glad he did. Daddy and Vicky just stared at me.

"You said there would be kids my age," I said to Daddy, and then I got it. The kid my age could be a boy. From the looks on their faces, I realized the kid my age could be Ben, and he didn't look any happier about it than I was.

"My, you're tall for ten years old, aren't you?" Vicky said, as if she'd never seen me before.

"I'm going to be eleven," I said, "in twenty-three days."

"You take after your daddy, I guess," Vicky said. "Those long legs."

"Mom is taller than Daddy," I said. "In her bare feet."

Vicky crossed her arms over her chest and shot Daddy a worried look. I could hear Harris's truck noises from inside the house.

"Well, why don't we figure out where everybody sleeps?" Daddy said. He hurried into the house without letting Vicky go first or anything polite like that. Ben let us go first, or at least he wasn't in a big hurry.

We found Harris jumping on my bed, saying *vroom* every time he lifted into the air. Since everyone was looking at him, he worked at jumping higher.

I'm not allowed to jump on the bed.

"This is my room," I said, hoping Daddy would make him stop.

Daddy cleared his throat. "I thought we might give this room to the boys, since it has two beds," he said. Harris stopped jumping to listen in. I mean, his motor was sort of rumbling, but he was listening.

Me too.

I figured that left two bedrooms and a lumpy pullout couch in what we called the family room. This is a wide spot as you go through the house, where all the rooms with doors open up, including the bathroom. No privacy at all.

And one of those bedrooms had the bed Mom and Daddy used to sleep in. I felt my eyebrows pull together in a frown.

Vicky said, "Um, Harris sleeps with me when he's in a strange place. So it's the sofa bed for us?"

"You'd better take my—uh, the double bed," Daddy said.

"Are you sure?" Vicky asked.

"Of course," Daddy said.

Ben had been looking through the rooms while they talked. "If Lexie takes that room with the single bed, I can bunk in here with Jim. Then nobody has to sleep on the couch."

Now he was calling my daddy Jim. I didn't like it that he sounded like he'd known Daddy longer than I had.

"We'll have to clear some junk out of there, though," Ben added, "if that's where Lexie's sleeping."

"That's not junk, that's the deck furniture," Daddy said. He looked a little sunburned.

Five

I also didn't like to have Ben deciding where I'd sleep. The two "big" bedrooms in the shore house were smaller than my room at home. The room he was talking about was the size of a closet. And the window wall slanted so that I had to walk bent over in half the room. The bed in there was my old junior bed.

"Lexie?" Daddy said. His voice went with the words, *Are you my big girl or are you still a baby?*

I wanted to be a baby but it felt too late for that. I had already gotten too grown up. I really didn't want to share with anyone and I didn't want to end up on the couch either.

"Okay," I said. It seemed the best way to fit everyone in and I still had my own room.

"That's okay, then," Daddy said. He looked relieved. When Harris gave a little jump, Daddy pretended not to see. "I'll help Ben bring your things in, okay?"

Harris started jumping again.

Vicky had left some stuff on the table as she'd come through the house. "I guess we ought to put away the groceries," she said, still like she was talking to the room.

Harris went on jumping. I didn't think I should be the one to tell him about the rules around here. Or Vicky either.

Vicky and I walked back to the kitchen. When she opened the fridge, she made a face. "Mom wasn't here to clean it up last summer," I said. "She always left it clean, clean, clean."

"That's okay, Lexie," she said. "With two boys I've learned to live with a little fuzzy ketchup." She left her groceries in the bag, like Daddy did, as she put them in the fridge.

"It's probably a good idea if I give your dad a

hand," she said. "Where can I find sheets for the beds?"

I showed her the space over the water heater, where a lot of sheets and towels and pillows were stuffed. They smelled like the house. "Mom usually washes all of them before we use them."

She looked into the washer. "Daddy hasn't gotten around to it yet," I said.

"I'll do it," Vicky said, and pulled down a few more sheets to stuff into the wash. She added soap and turned on the machine.

We heard a loud thump from my bedroom. From my old bedroom. Vicky dropped the soap box and ran. I stayed right behind her. We found Harris sitting on the floor next to the bed, his mouth so wide open I could have counted all his teeth.

He caught his breath and let out a loud wail.

He'd slipped off the bed, the way I'd done that time when I was little. I bit my lip and it bled all over the place. I had to eat baby food for days to keep it from starting up again.

He sure could yell. Vicky picked him up and sat on the bed and rocked him, crooning over him. Harris's face had turned beet red. But he wasn't bleeding and he didn't look broken, the first things Mom always checks. He looked like he would live.

Daddy hurried in from outside, still holding a suitcase.

"He jumped too close to the edge of the bed," I said. Loudly.

Daddy frowned. He said, "That's why we don't jump on beds around here." He'd lost the polite voice he'd been using and sounded pretty much the way he did that time I'd slipped off the bed the same way. He sounded like he meant *And that's final*.

He put Vicky's suitcase in the other bedroom. Then he went straight back out to the car. She kept looking at the door as if she expected him to pop back in and say something. Like, he didn't mean to sound so final.

Now I felt bad, because I didn't tell her the rule.

"I'm sure he knew Harris is going to be all right," I said, to smooth things over. It wasn't that I wanted to have her here. In fact, I hoped she would turn out not to like the shore very much. Now that she was here, I'd rather she and

Daddy didn't fight. She gave me a look that said pretty much the same thing.

She bounced Harris on her lap and told him some baby rhyming story about his toes, Moses supposes da da da da da, but Moses supposes dadadadada, something like that. She kept saying it over and over, until Harris stopped crying so hard. He looked sleepy.

I went to the window to see if Daddy was bringing more stuff in. He and Ben were walking around in the high grass, Daddy pointing first one way and then the other. It bothered me that he'd gone walking with Ben and didn't ask me to come along.

Harris wriggled off Vicky's lap and started his motor. She let him go, saying, "We ought to get these beds made up. We'll do another wash tomorrow."

Vicky brought some sheets back to the bedroom and I helped her sort out which ones went on which bed. She was kind of quiet, like she was worried that Harris would get on Daddy's nerves.

Or maybe she thought Daddy should have been in here giving *her* a hand. Maybe she and

Daddy were about to have a fight. Maybe she was working out what she would say if they did. I began to get a knot in my stomach.

Harris ran around making truck sounds. Speeding trucks, coming-to-a-fast-stop trucks, crashing trucks. I figured he was embarrassed about falling off the bed and now he wanted to show us what an excellent truck he was.

After we finished one bed, Vicky went out to the porch and yelled for Ben to bring the rest of their stuff from the car. While we made the beds, Ben and Daddy made several trips.

Vicky brought a lot more stuff than we did. "How long are you staying?" I asked.

"Just the week," Vicky said in this bright cheerful voice that still sounded a lot like Mary's.

"Me too," I told her. "I didn't need this much stuff."

"That's because you knew what you needed," Vicky said. "I'll know better next time."

She looked at me right after saying this and then looked away very quickly. Twice. Two quick looks.

I knew now. She expected to come here again this summer. Probably every weekend. I wasn't going to have a single weekend with Daddy. Not by myself, anyway.

Not unless Harris was a real pain in the neck. I hoped he would be.

Daddy put his head into the bedroom and said, "We got all the deck furniture out of your room, Lexie."

I didn't say anything. But that wasn't my room.

With all the deck furniture out, I could sit on the junior bed. It was hard. And there wasn't any lamp to read by.

I pulled and shoved the bed over so I could turn out the ceiling light without getting up. Now the bed took up most of the space where I could stand straight. I didn't care.

Daddy looked in. "This looks, um, cozy." He had his polite voice back in working order.

"I don't like to get out of bed to turn off the light," I said.

Daddy had already turned his head to talk to Vicky. He said, "There's a nice little bar and grill down on the pier."

Vicky didn't act like they'd been fighting. "That sounds wonderful," she said.

The knot in my stomach let go. I hadn't known until right then how much I'd been dreading a fight. Even if it meant that Vicky would pack up her boys and go, I was dreading it.

"Let's go get a real meal," Daddy said. "Grab a sweater, Lexie. The boys will need jackets when the sun goes down, Vicky."

I could eat a real meal. We'd left our sandwiches out on the deck. The seagulls would come along and clean up after us, Daddy always said.

I got my suitcase and brought it back to that tiny room that was not my room so I could dig through it without having to worry about my underwear falling out in front of everyone or something.

Mom didn't pack a sweater, only a sweatshirt. I set out my book with the pink cover so it would feel a little bit like my room when I got back. Mom said that book always reminded her why people came to the beach. It's fun to read a book with pictures. And it reminded me to use sunscreen.

I could hear the others saying they were ready. I tied the sweatshirt around my waist in a hurry. Then I dug through my duffel bag for my baseball cap. I put it on backward and ran outside.

I was the last one out. So I didn't know Ben had put on a baseball cap. Backward. We looked at each other and didn't say anything. After a moment, he took off his cap and threw it onto the backseat of his mother's car.

Vicky grabbed him around and gave him a big hug. She meant she loved him but she also hoped he wasn't going to make trouble. Mothers have their own language of hugs.

Six

We rode in Vicky's car, which was sort of horrible. Not just because the car was awfully hot but because I sat with the boys. Vicky said, "You look like a happy family back here," as she strapped Harris into his car seat. None of us answered her.

Ben sat next to the window, like he thought he'd get cooties from sitting next to me. I stayed in the middle, because I didn't want to sit very next to Harris, who was driving a pretty spitty truck to the restaurant.

His car seat came with a steering wheel and plastic keys and a stick shift that made a grating noise right in my ear. Twice I had to wipe a little spray of spit off my arm with my sweatshirt.

At dinner, Daddy still acted polite. He put Harris next to Vicky. Ben took the seat on the other side of Daddy, so I sat across from Ben.

Really, I didn't mind that I didn't get to sit beside Daddy. I was glad I didn't have to sit with Harris in case he turned out to be a messy eater.

I scooted my chair to the side nearest Vicky so Ben wouldn't have to worry about the cooties. Harris wouldn't sit in a booster chair, so I could only see him from above the little dent in his chin. We all knew he was there. He made quiet little motor noises while we waited for the waitress.

Daddy asked the boys what they wanted to order, the way he never asked me. "Anything fried for Mack," Ben said. "His taste buds aren't fully formed yet. He'll eat octopus brains so long as they're fried in batter." He made it sound as if his little brother didn't know any better.

Harris's eyes went puppy sad.

"Good for him," Daddy said. "Octopus brains are one of my big favorites." Harris perked right up again.

I was sort of proud of Daddy for making

Harris feel better. I started teasing him anyway. "Daddy's taste buds aren't either, what you said, formed."

Harris said, "Haaah." It took me a second to know he was laughing.

Vicky brushed her hand over his head, messing up his hair. "Silly boy," she said. And she smiled at me like I'd helped make him feel like he was included in a big boy club.

Ben said, "I'll have the surf and turf."

"Me too," I said before Daddy could tell me what I wanted. I love the surf and turf picture on the menu.

"That isn't what you usually order," Daddy said.

"I want something different," I said. I looked up in time to see this little smile flit over Ben's face. He thought I ordered surf and turf because he'd ordered it.

I felt my face go all hot. I wore my cap backward and now I'd ordered the same thing he did and he thought it was because, well, just because. The way Vicky smiled, I knew she thought so too.

"I changed my mind," I said in a hurry. "I'll have the crab cakes."

"I think you'd better have the fried shrimp, the way you always do," Daddy said.

"I want the crab cakes."

"Me too," Harris said in a deep voice. It was the first thing I'd heard him say that didn't sound like a truck. I didn't know he could talk.

"They aren't the kind of cake you think," Vicky said to him.

"Me too," Harris said again.

"That's it," I said, closing the menu. I didn't mind if he copied me. "We're decided."

"Mack," Vicky said, "crab cakes don't come as a child's meal."

"It's okay," Daddy said. "Two or three crab cakes isn't that much. I'll eat one if there's a leftover."

The corners of Harris's mouth turned up. Vicky shrugged, but I thought she liked Daddy's answer too.

The restaurant was awfully busy, and it wasn't our turn to be served for the longest time. Vicky asked Ben to take Harris to the restroom to wash his hands. He'd been washed right before we left the house. Stuff had already stuck to his fingers again.

I saw Ben didn't mind holding one of those

furry hands as he took Harris off to the restroom. For a minute I felt bad for him. Then I
thought, He's Harris's big brother, probably he
had furry hands when he was little too. Furry
hands don't bother him.

Daddy and Vicky talked to each other while
the boys were gone, almost as if I wasn't there.

I didn't know why Daddy liked Vicky so
much. Everything about Mom looked better to
me. And Mom would have talked to me sometimes, because that's good manners.

I fiddled with my silverware until the knife hit
my water glass and made a noise that hurt my ears.
Daddy gave me a look that meant *Settle down.*

I was glad when the boys came back. Harris
purred along on his own, no conversation there,
and Ben and I tried not to look at each other. We
mostly read our menus all over again. Still, it
wasn't as bad as being alone with Daddy and Vicky.

Whenever a waitress passed our table, which
was pretty often, Harris revved his motor louder.
Daddy said, "The service is usually much better
here."

Another waitress went by and Harris revved
his motor again. *Really* loud. Two waitresses

looked our way, and one of them walked over. Either it was finally our turn or they got tired of being revved at.

Daddy ordered two crab cake baskets and three surf and turf dinners. Ben said, "You know, those crab cakes sound really good. Think I'll change my order to that."

When I looked at him, he grinned. I stared. It was like finding out Harris could talk. I was so overwhelmed I didn't smile back.

Then Harris spilled his water all over the tablecloth.

Daddy leaped up as if the water had gone into his lap. Vicky leaped up too, blotting furiously with her napkin, trying to stop the water from soaking the tablecloth. Daddy dropped his napkin over the spill.

"Are you wet?" Vicky asked him.

"No."

Vicky sat down. "We don't really need to get all excited, then," she said. "It's just the tablecloth. And it's just water."

Daddy sat down, clearing his throat a little.

It left us with a funny feeling over the table, the air felt sort of tight. I thought it might help if someone said something. Like *Daddy's not that good with spills and stuff.*

I couldn't make myself say it.

Up until now, Ben had ignored the whole thing, like he was sitting at somebody else's table. He'd gone very still, watching his mother.

Vicky took care of it. "I'm so glad you asked us out to your place," she said to Daddy. "It's a new experience for us."

"The shore?" He looked shocked. "You've never been to the shore?"

"Not since Ben was too little to remember it," Vicky said happily. She made it sound like she chirped. I guess it cheered her up to have the right thing to say.

Daddy kept looking at her like he couldn't imagine someone not coming to the shore every weekend. She added, "Well, I can't swim, have I mentioned that?"

Daddy asked, "How about Ben and Harris?"

Vicky gave a little shrug and sighed. I took that for *no.*

"Does anybody else feel kind of itchy?" Ben asked. He reached down to scratch his leg.

Seven

"*Itchy?*" Vicky *said.* "You feel itchy?"

"It's not bad," Ben said. "Maybe I got into some poison ivy."

"You probably got a mosquito bite," I said. I could get itchy just thinking about it. "Mosquitoes come out early when they haven't eaten all winter."

Daddy and Vicky laughed like I'd said something cute. "Those aren't last year's mosquitoes, Lexie," Daddy said. "It's all new mosquitoes this year."

I didn't see that it mattered. Old or new, they were pretty hungry when people first arrived at the shore.

"I felt like *I* might have gotten a bite or two,"

Vicky said. "Oh, look, our dinners are coming."

The sides of the basket were too high for Harris to see what he had in there. He felt around, nearly spilling his basket. Vicky set a crab cake on a bread plate for him.

Harris ate with his fingers. He crumbled everything up before he ate it. And he wanted ketchup on everything, the crab cakes and the fries *and* the coleslaw in the creamy sauce.

Vicky didn't seem to notice that it bothered Daddy that Harris ate with his fingers. All the time she was fixing stuff for Harris, she talked about her sister, who was getting married.

I bet Daddy didn't hear a word she said. I think he was trying not to look at Harris. I couldn't figure out how Harris kept his motor going while he chewed.

Vicky didn't see that Ben kept scratching his bites. Once I thought Vicky reached down to scratch a bite, but she might have been straightening her skirt.

Mainly I ate my dinner. A couple of handfuls of chips and part of a turkey sandwich were all I had gotten since breakfast and I was hungry. I used a fork, even for my fries.

I didn't want to look at Harris anyway. He kept going back to feeling around in the basket with his messy hands, like there might be something he'd missed. The whole basket had ketchup and creamy sauce splotches. The waitress was going to have to throw it out.

Daddy looked like he was listening hard to all this boring stuff about the wedding plans. Probably he was thinking about that leftover crab cake he'd promised to eat. He nodded a lot. It was only when he nodded at something when he should have shaken his head, like *oh, no,* that Vicky stopped talking about her sister's wedding.

"Yikes!" Ben said.

I stared at him. Who says *yikes*?

He stared at his legs under the table edge like they belonged to someone else. Vicky and Daddy went right on talking. Suddenly, he scooted his chair back. "There's another one."

"Another what?" Vicky asked in an irritated way. Like she thought he was about to be rude or something.

"Bug," Ben said.

Vicky said, "Ben." Very no-nonsense.

He stood up. There were red marks on his

legs where he'd been scratching, but no mosquito bites. Vicky looked startled now. I figured I knew what it was. I wasn't saying a word.

Daddy wasn't saying a word either.

Ben said, "Not a big bug, a flea. Fleas, like on a dog."

"Where?" Vicky asked.

"On me," he said. "There are fleas on me."

"I doubt they're fleas," Vicky said. She reached down and scratched.

Daddy cleared his throat. "It's possible," he said, "that Ben picked up sand fleas out in the grass."

"Sand fleas?" Vicky said.

"Mom always gets about a hundred bites," I said. I would have added that they always made her swell up and itch for days but Daddy interrupted.

"It's nothing," Daddy said. "I usually spray around the house to kill them off. I'll do it tomorrow and we won't be bothered."

"Oh. Okay." Vicky gave another good scratch. "You were out in the grass too."

"Nothing bites me," Daddy said. "Not fleas, not mosquitoes, not dogs."

"Lucky you," Ben muttered.

"What do you think about dessert?" Daddy asked.

Harris didn't pick up a fork or a spoon once. Although he did let his motor die out when he got chocolate cake.

I was glad I wasn't sitting next to him. I could see Daddy wanting to show him how to use the utensils. Then he looked over at somebody else's table. I figured the utensils would come tomorrow.

When Harris finished eating, he started his motor. "Put, vut, vrrm, vroom," he said. Vicky eyed him the way Mom eyes my plate to decide whether I've eaten enough. Vicky said, "Ben, would you help your brother?"

She meant wash his hands again, which he needed now more than before. When Ben got up, we saw how red his legs had gotten from scratching. The sand fleas had given him a rash.

"Good heavens," Vicky said, looking him over. "Sand fleas?"

Ben looked a little alarmed himself.

Daddy said, "He must be one of those people who have a big reaction to them. We'll stop at the drugstore on the way home and get some Benadryl. He'll be good as new in the morning."

When we got up to leave, Vicky lifted her skirt a little to go down the stairs at the front of the restaurant. She had a blotchy red rash too.

Eight

Harris fell asleep on the ride home, and woke up as Vicky carried him inside. He had to get down immediately and start his motor. He had engine trouble all the way up the stairs.

Vicky said, "Ben, let's get that stuff on your legs."

Daddy handed Ben the plastic bag with the calamine lotion and the Benadryl.

Vicky looked like she would go into the bathroom with Ben. "I don't need help," he said.

"You have to get the backs of your legs," she said.

"I can do it," Ben said.

"He can manage," Daddy said. "He's fourteen years old. Practically a man."

Harris stood there with his motor humming and his face turned up, waiting to see how everything was going to turn out. A truck waiting for the traffic lights to change.

"Don't be long," Vicky said with a sigh. "I need to use that stuff too."

Ben looked at his mother and she raised her skirt to her knees. Her legs were red and puffier-looking than his, although she hadn't scratched as much. I was pretty sure she didn't have puffy legs before.

"All right," he said, giving in. "Come on."

Harris wouldn't be left behind. The three of them could hardly fit in that tiny bathroom. We listened to Vicky getting Harris to stand in the shower stall.

"It's too wet."

"We won't turn on the water."

"Wet."

It took a while to convince him he wasn't going to have to take a shower. I flopped down in a wicker chair and stared at the door. Daddy sat down on the sofa and looked at me with what Mom calls his sheepdog look. He used it whenever he disappointed her. I hoped he wouldn't start saving that look for me.

He kept the same face going, expecting me to say something nice. Everything we said could be heard inside the bathroom. And everything they said could be heard where we were.

"You sit on the seat, Ben," Vicky was saying. "You'll be able to reach the backs of your legs easiest that way. We have to make sure we cover all the skin."

"Harris, quit squeezing the cotton balls," Ben said. "They're sticking to you."

"Harris," Vicky whined. And then she said in an annoyed tone, "His hands were clean before we left the restaurant. What did he touch that was sticky? That's what I want to know."

"Stickiness just oozes from his pores," Ben said, making me grin. I listened to the sounds of brakes screeching and water running in the sink, and then a few minutes of quiet busyness.

I saw out of the corner of my eye that Daddy had seen me grin. I knew he wanted me to look at him and smile. I stared at the picture over his head, a picture of three pots of geraniums. He'd ruined my vacation.

I didn't want to sit there with him any longer. I could go read my book or I could go out on the deck.

I heard Ben ask his mother, "Did you see these shore houses are kind of run down? Especially this one."

"It needs a paint job," Vicky told him.

We painted the porch last summer, I thought as if I was telling them. Daddy did it right before Mom and I left. Then he came home and moved out of the house in Baltimore.

Which reminded me all the more that this would be our first summer of weekends here together alone. At least, it was supposed to be.

"It's like this house was built by one of the three little pigs," Ben said. I glanced at Daddy to see how he was taking this.

He looked like he might have some bites too, but not from fleas.

Ben said, "Even with a paint job—"

"Benjamin, you're dripping all over the floor," Vicky said.

"Harris is dropping cotton balls on the floor," Ben said.

"Harris, cut that out," Vicky said.

"With a paint job, this is still a shack," Ben said.

"It's a very expensive shack," Daddy said as if Ben stood in the room with us. There was a kind of dead moment when I think nobody moved, nobody breathed. Not even Harris.

Then from the bathroom came a sound like a hissy fit, the kind a cat has right before it scratches. It had to be Vicky.

"I apologize," Ben said loudly. "It was only an observation."

Nine

I went out to stand on the deck. After a minute, Daddy came out there too. "I want you to get to know them," Daddy said.

"I don't need to know them," I said.

I heard nothing then but the sound of the water. Slap, lap. Until Daddy said, "Look, water fairies."

I looked where he pointed and saw light flashing under the water. White and green mostly, bits of blue and purple. Like light dancing there. When I was little, Mom and I used to say those were water fairies. Daddy told me what they really were.

"Those are schools of fish with tiny, tiny animals clinging to them," I told him. "Tiny little animals with specks of light like lightning bugs. I don't like fairy tales anymore."

Vicky came out then. I moved down to the other end of the deck and stared out to sea. I listened to Daddy tell Ben and Harris about the little animals. He didn't say anything about water fairies.

Ben asked some questions, like did we ever see sharks or dolphins around here. He sounded pretty excited about being near the ocean, and for a minute, I could forget I didn't want him here.

Between Ben's questions, Vicky said how wonderful the air felt, how beautiful the stars were, how special the world was. Mary Tyler Moore doesn't come up with such a lot of dumb remarks. Well, she does, but she doesn't make them all at once.

I looked at all of them standing together, outlined on one side by the little bit of yellow light that filtered out from the house and on the other side by the silver light of the moon.

I thought about how if Daddy ever married

Vicky, it would always be like this. Vicky and the boys would stay out here like Mom and I did. When Daddy came on the weekend they would be a whole family, and when I came, I would be a guest.

Harris stood beside Vicky, his hair standing up a little in the wind, his motor humming. "Well, Harris, it must be way past your bedtime," Daddy said.

Harris didn't even gun his motor.

"It is getting late," Vicky said, sounding more helpless than ever. "I got up awfully early this morning."

"Oh, I didn't mean—" Daddy said.

"I always rub his back until he falls asleep," Vicky said. "I ought to be there if he wakes up."

"Once he's asleep, he won't wake up," Daddy said hopefully. "The sea air and all."

"You know what they say," Vicky said with a little laugh. "Early to bed, early to rise."

"Doesn't leave much possibility for nightlife," Daddy said.

Vicky looked at him the way Mom sometimes does.

"Well, it's fine really," Daddy said, sounding like somebody who'd lost a game.

"Ben, you were up so early this morning . . . ," Vicky began.

I knew how that speech ended. Ben was already on his way inside. Vicky went too, saying, "I want to wash Harris's hands, that's all. No baths tonight."

"You mean showers," Ben said. "No bathtub."

"Ben!" Vicky said like she was shushing him.

After a moment I was alone with Daddy.

No one said good night to me. They'd probably already forgotten I was there. Of course, they didn't really say good night to Daddy either. Not everybody was like my mom, who tried to make everyone feel noticed.

"Just you and me, Lex," Daddy said.

"I'm going to bed," I said. I could read my book all the way to the end. I didn't want Daddy to spend time with me because everybody else had another place to be. He could only spend time with me if he thought of me first.

I missed Mom a whole lot right then. I wanted to call her. But there isn't one place to stand in the shore house where everybody else can't hear what you're saying.

Plus I didn't know what I would say.

Except that weekends at the shore were not going to be nearly as much fun as they had been last year. And even then, they weren't all that great.

Ten

Here's a horrible thing about boys. They leave toilet seats up and a person can fall in if she's not careful, especially in the middle of the night.

Here's a horrible thing about Ben. He walks around while he's brushing his teeth in the morning, sort of foaming at the mouth. Then he leaves his toothbrush in the sink, still foaming a little all by itself. Horrible.

Somebody had pulled the table into the middle of the floor again so there was room for five chairs. Daddy came in from the deck and sat down at one end. Holding my breath, I took the chair across from the two together.

Vicky brought the frying pan over and put eggs on all the plates but one. She pointed to one of the two chairs. "Mack, you sit right here so you'll be next to me."

Whew.

He climbed up and looked around at everybody's plates while he was sitting on his knees. He had toast and bacon. He revved his motor and pointed to the eggs.

"Are you sure?" Vicky asked him, and he nodded so hard his motor choked a little.

She sighed and moved one of her fried eggs to Harris's plate. His motor settled right down. Vicky put the pan back on the stove and sat down. Ben came last and dove right in without waiting to see if we all had what we needed, if everybody was ready to eat.

Here's a horrible thing about Harris. He doesn't eat *egg yolk* with a fork. I watched because I wanted to know.

Really, he didn't eat the egg at all. While he ate the toast and bacon, he did a little finger painting with the yolk. Vicky and Ben were busy comparing their flea bites, or maybe they were used to him.

Daddy tried not to see what Harris was doing. He kept his newspaper folded so it fit next to his plate, and he pretended to read. I knew he was pretending because he never picked it up and turned the page and refolded it the way he usually would if he was reading.

"I could cut that for you, Harris," Daddy said when he couldn't pretend not to see this anymore. "You could eat it with a fork."

Harris's motor didn't hiccup.

"The yolk sticks between the tines," Daddy said as Harris squished some yolk together with some white. "A fork makes a real cool earth mover."

I felt a little smile in my heart, but it wasn't a very nice smile. It wasn't about Harris, it was about Daddy. He wouldn't be able to stand Harris for long.

"It's important to learn to use your utensils," Daddy said firmly.

Harris motored on as if he couldn't hear a word. And then he went around the plate and, with a little garbage-truck-like roar before each bite, ate the toast and bacon.

I was beginning to like Harris.

"I thought I'd walk along the shore," Ben said as he dropped his paper napkin on his empty plate. "Explore a little."

"I can show you," I said. I knew the shore by heart.

"I kind of wanted to go by myself," Ben said.

I wet my finger and picked up bacon crumbs from my plate. I knew what Ben was thinking. He didn't want to play with some little kid, especially a girl.

The table had gotten very quiet. Harris's motor had died out.

"It isn't exploring if somebody shows me, that's all," he said.

"I understand, Ben," Vicky said. "But you're Lexie's guest."

"No, he's not," I said, still not looking up. "He's Daddy's guest. If I'd known we could bring company, I would've brought some of my own."

"Lexie," Daddy said as if I was the one eating with my fingers. Well, I was, but not like Harris. I looked up through my eyelashes. Vicky looked at me in a certain way that knew a lot. It wasn't at all a mean look. That look gave me courage.

"I'm going beachcombing," I said to Ben. He

looked the same as the night before, hair tuft and parentheses. No earphones. "It's what I always do here. So I don't want you looking at me like you think I copied you or I'm following you, something stupid like that."

"Deal," Ben said.

I didn't know it could be that simple. I said what I wanted and he said okay. I tried to think why things had never seemed that easy before. I couldn't figure it out.

"Nobody goes into the water until we're out there with you," Vicky said.

"I can swim," I said. "I never go into deep water until Mo—somebody is watching."

"Do what you always do," Daddy said. "We'll be out there sunbathing in a few minutes. I hope we don't all have to draw up borders, like for territories."

"We'll get to sunbathing. There's some work needed in this kitchen first," Vicky said, looking right at Daddy. She didn't seem all that Mary Tyler Moore after all. Her flea bites were worse. Probably the puffy legs didn't make it easy to be chirpy.

Daddy laughed. "Okay, I guess it's first things

first." This was new, the way he gave in. Like somebody who was just learning the rules and was still cheerful about his mistakes. "It's the *shore,* Vicky. I get like a kid out here."

That was what Mom used to say, that he got like a kid out here. But he'd never laughed when she said it. He'd never stayed to help with the dishes either.

I hadn't quite finished my breakfast when Ben got up to go out. I pushed away from the table. This was still my shore. I got to pick which part of it was mine to explore first. I stopped at the bottom of the steps to scan the sandy beach both ways. I took my time. Mainly I had to watch for messy spots.

Ben looked both ways like someone crossing the street in traffic.

He didn't know what to look for. And I couldn't really tell him. I never knew what I might find. There were always lots of seaweed and creatures like starfish and jellyfish and sea urchins. Well, not so many starfish and sea urchins actually washed up.

But there was always something interesting.

"I'm going this way," I told Ben, pointing. I

took the big rusty bucket I used for collecting and a shovel from a hook under the deck, right where I always left it. I poured a little water out of the bucket and I was ready to go.

I left him standing there. With that hair tuft and the parentheses, and wearing the baggy shorts over his skinny legs, he didn't look much like an explorer to me. He looked like a Muppet who'd lost his skateboard.

Eleven

I spent the first ten minutes walking straight away from the house, not looking at anything. Mostly I walked where the sand was still wet and almost solid under my feet, because I could walk fast.

I passed up the bird footprints that would get washed away and several other things that looked interesting. Empty bottles, a wooden crate with a mermaid on the label, an oar.

I wanted to have as much of the shore as possible to call my own. I didn't want Ben circling around and showing up four or five houses away and saying that was his territory to explore.

One boy I knew was really sneaky enough to

do that, but he was back home in Baltimore. I didn't know yet if Ben could be sneaky. I didn't want to take chances.

There weren't too many people outside. The water looked a little rough today. It rushed onto the shore, soaking in fast and leaving a white foam on the sand for a few seconds before that disappeared too.

I remembered I still hadn't called my mom. I couldn't do it with Harris putt-putting around. Worse, what if Vicky said something and Mom said, *Whose voice is that?* What would I tell her?

I still had all day to call, that part didn't worry me. I tried to think of how I could get the house to myself. Maybe I could ask Daddy to take everybody outside.

When I looked back, I was about twenty houses away from ours. I could see Ben, still hanging around the steps. I relaxed and wandered into the surf, letting the cold water wash up over my ankles. The first splash felt like a shock. I got used to that fast.

I decided it was good enough being at the

shore this morning, even if it wasn't going to be Daddy and me. Wet sand scrunched up between my toes, and wind blew my hair all around, and the sun felt warm on my shoulders. I had my bathing suit on under my shorts and T-shirt so I could get wet if the sun got too hot.

Mrs. Brady's little pink poodle barked at me. Apricot poodle, Mrs. Brady says, but that poodle looks pink to me. Its name is Prissy.

Mrs. Brady was one of the beach people who came back to their houses each year. She always got here before we did. And she walked along the beach every day.

A lot of the houses had different people each summer, some were different every week. Sometimes there were other kids to play with. It always took a few days to get to know everybody.

I found a starfish. A real starfish with one leg missing. Dead. It was still an interesting find. I shoveled some sand over it. And I found a bed of clams. The way to tell is by all the little holes in the sand where they suck in air to breathe.

When I was little, Daddy used to tell me that if I put my toes over the holes I would be able to

feel them breathe—thoop, thoop, thoop—
against my skin. I didn't think I really could, but
hearing those words, thoop, thoop, thoop, gave
me such a thrill all over I could hardly stand it. I
put my toes over the holes as I walked.

Finally, I'd staked out enough territory. I
stopped trying to get so far from the house and
I started to look for beach glass and anything
else good that had washed up on the sand.

I came across this wonderful tangle of fishing
line and hooks. The water had wrapped the
whole mess around a piece of twisted metal and
trapped one tiny perfect spiral shell inside like it
was in an aquarium. When I shook it, the shell
moved but it didn't fall out.

I put it in my bucket.

I started back, going slowly now. It felt good
to wander in and out of the surf, getting sand on
my feet and letting the water wash it off.

I investigated every piece of trash I'd passed
before. I kept a bottle that had writing in a for-
eign language.

And a thin wooden sign, a label really, that
could be peeled away from the rougher wood of
the crate. I got a splinter. It was worth it. The

mermaid looked like one might really look, kind of fishy.

And a piece of driftwood worn pale and smooth during a long voyage from wherever.

All the time, I kept my eyes peeled for a hermit crab. I looked under everything, poking around in some disgusting stuff because, hey, what do hermit crabs like to eat, right?

No luck there.

When I got about halfway home, I saw Ben running toward me. He didn't stop running even after he knew I had seen him. He was out of breath when he reached me.

"Shark," he wheezed as he came to a stop.

"Shark?"

He nodded and took the driftwood from me. He was all out of breath and still willing to carry the heaviest thing to hurry me along. I was happy to have some help. I didn't tell him it wasn't likely he'd seen a shark. Or a dolphin.

When he got his breath back, I asked, "Why didn't you go get your mom?"

"They went to the drugstore," Ben said. "Mom's bites are worse, she needs stronger medicine. You were so far off they figured they'd get back before you knew they were gone."

"So where'd you see this shark?"

"Wait, you'll see."

I dropped my bucket under the deck and out of the sun once we reached the house. I took the mermaid label and the fishing line piece upstairs and set them on the shelf with my collection. The bottles and driftwood could wait.

"Hurry up," Ben called to me.

"I'm coming."

We walked for five minutes in the other direction, going around a little bend in the land. Until last year, Mom never allowed me to walk out of sight by myself. We'd always walked this way together.

There was this one little section of shore behind a ridge of land. When the tide went out, some water got caught there, making a pool. When I was little, too little to go out in the water because it felt too rough, I played there every morning while Mom lay on a towel in the sand.

By the time we reached the tide pool, I knew what we would find.

"It's a shark," Ben said, stopping not too close to the edge. It swam slow circles around the pool as we watched. "A real shark."

It was a sand shark. No big deal. Then I remembered how excited I'd been the first time I found a sand shark. It was a big deal. A really big deal. Like the most exciting weekend I had all summer.

I didn't tell Ben. I didn't want to spoil it for him. Besides, it was a pretty big sand shark. As the shark swam around and around, the fin rode the water like a sailboat. "Wow," I said.

"Yeah," Ben said. "Lucky we found it before somebody got attacked or something."

It was big, but it wasn't that big. If we got Harris to lie down next to it, they'd probably be the same size. Except Harris would be wider.

It occurred to me that Ben might think I didn't know a sand shark when I saw it. He might be playing a joke on me. I squinted at him because he stood so the sun was in my eyes. He looked serious.

I said, "Maybe we should let it go."

He looked at me like I might be crazy. "Free the shark?"

Twelve

"Free the shark," I said.

"Who-oa."

I waited.

"How?" he said. "I mean, my mother will never forgive me if I let you get chewed."

I was glad to hear it. "I guess we ought to dig a canal," I said.

The look on his face told me everything.

I could see he thought it was a pretty good idea, although he didn't say so. In fact, I liked it better that he didn't feel like he had to say so.

I could see he hadn't expected me to come up with a good idea.

"We'll have to leave a kind of dam for the water," Ben said, beginning to take charge. "So the really dangerous moment is when we open the pool to the canal."

I looked at the sand shark lazily cruising the pool. I didn't think we were in too much danger. Ben and I started to dig. We could have gone back for shovels, I guess, but this frenzy to free the shark gripped us both. We dug with our hands, with clamshells, and with a piece of driftwood that was shaped like a big flat sandal. It was hot work.

We dug for a long time and two people walked by. Both times, it went the same way.

Ben said, "Quick, stand so she doesn't see the shark."

"It's only Mrs. Lee."

"Stand with your back to the pool," Ben said, "and try to look natural."

"Why?"

"It's a shark, that's why," he said. "It isn't like people love sharks. They might kill it."

"Some might," I agreed. Sand sharks make pretty good eating. I didn't want to see that happen to this one, though. I'd begun to feel the way I'd feel toward a stray dog, like we had to protect it. "Mrs. Lee wouldn't kill it, though."

"Wave," he said, because Mrs. Lee was waving.

Ben did this because he was brave and still hadn't figured out that the shark wouldn't try to eat him. I did it because I didn't want someone to come up to Ben and say, "Oh, it's a sand shark. They hardly ever bite."

"Don't back up any more," he said. "You're getting too close to the pool's edge. Sharks jump out of the water, you know."

I waved long and hard at Mrs. Lee. It was a break from the digging. I couldn't work as hard as Ben. I didn't want to admit maybe I couldn't work as long either.

When he went back to digging, so did I. After a while, we were close enough to the ocean that each time a wave washed in, water filled the end of the canal and wet our legs. The water drained quickly as the wave slid away, leaving us feeling cool enough to keep on.

"We have a problem," Ben said as we neared the water.

I sat in the canal, pushing sand ahead of me with my feet, mainly because my arms were tired. "What's that?"

"This canal is long."

"So?"

"So there may not be enough water in that pool to carry him all the way out to sea."

"Huh?"

"The water from the pool is going to spread out along this canal," Ben explained. "Some of it may soak in. He could get stuck halfway to the water's edge. Beached."

I still wasn't worried. We could pick up that shark by the tail and pull it to the water. Ben didn't know this, of course. I asked, "What do you think we ought to do?"

"Digging deeper might help," he said.

I lay back in the canal and wondered how to tell him about sand sharks. I thought maybe I should get Daddy to tell him, and I could pretend I didn't know either. That seemed like a good plan. Only I was too tired to walk all the way back to the house.

"If we dig deep enough," he said, still figuring

things out, "the ocean might come to him."

Well, that was it, of course. "We could wait," I said. "The tide will come in again."

"I knew that," Ben said. He looked tired too, but he didn't stop digging, not until we finished.

We stood up and let our arms hang at our sides as we stared out at the ocean for a while. My arms felt too heavy to lift and maybe Ben's did too, because we moved up the shore to think the situation over some more. At least, that was what Ben said we were doing. I was resting.

We sat close enough to study the shark. It seemed to be studying us back. "Maybe we should move further away," Ben said. "It's looking right at us."

I didn't move. "I saw a big shark's eyes up close once at the aquarium," I said. "They don't really seem to look at anything. I mean, they must, but their eyes are so flat or something, it's too weird. I bet we look like paper dolls to them."

"You might be right," Ben said. "Did you know that flies see hundreds of you when they look at you?"

"Hundreds?"

"Well. Thirty or so, at least," he said. "And chameleons are stranger. They can see you from two angles at the same time."

"You got that off the science channel?"

"Science class. I bet that water's getting too warm." I could hear him thinking up more work for us to do. He added, "Maybe we ought to bucket some cool water in to him."

"I'm getting hungry." I sort of hoped he'd volunteer to go back and get us some lunch.

Ben looked at me the way he'd been looking at the shark. "You're getting sunburned."

I didn't feel it till he brought it up. I'd forgotten to put on the sunscreen.

I remembered Ben had gotten pink at first. Now he looked brown all over. "I shouldn't have kept you out here working like this," he said.

I was only a little kid, that was what he really meant. "I can stay as long as you can."

"We dug a hundred feet, I bet," he said.

I didn't say anything to this. I heard his stomach growl.

There were people out on their decks, firing

94

up grills. Also, there were a few sunbathers and a couple of swimmers out in the water. We'd been so busy I'd hardly looked at anybody else.

"You could go back long enough to eat," he said in that same voice he used with Harris. "You can bring something back for me."

He wouldn't argue with me, which was okay. I didn't really want to fight. I didn't like to be treated like I was no more grown up than Harris either.

"Nope," I said. I lay back in the sand, wet and cool.

"Girls are so stubborn," he said in pretty much the same tone he used when he talked about the shark.

I waited to see how that felt. It didn't bother me.

"I'll go back and get buckets and something for us to eat," he said, getting up.

"I'll come with you," I said. I had to get my own lunch if I didn't want to look like a little kid.

"Somebody has to stand guard over the shark."

Thirteen

He had a point. In case someone thought the shark could be dangerous, or in danger, it needed a guard. "Okay, so I'll go back for buckets and lunch," I said. "You're a better guard."

I trudged back to the house. Once I was up and moving, I wasn't so tired. I found Daddy in the kitchen with Harris. Daddy didn't look as happy about this as Harris did. Probably I didn't either.

"What're you guys doing in here?"

Daddy made a pile of potato chips next to his tuna sandwich. "Harris needs time to get used to new places."

There was a plastic road map spread out on the table. Harris had a bunch of tiny cars that he moved along the roads, making motor noises for each one.

"He doesn't like to go outside much right at first," Daddy said. "Maybe later."

I looked at Harris. He wore a pair of swim trunks and no shirt, a little boy practicing for going to the shore.

"Where's Vicky?" I asked. The food was on the table. I started to make sandwiches for Ben and me.

"The stuff she took made her sleepy. Where's Ben?"

I waved a hand toward the shore. I wanted to talk to Daddy. It was going to be harder with Harris listening in. I was pretty sure Harris was smarter than he looked.

"No turkey?" I asked.

"Vicky finished it off," he said. "That allergy medicine made her hungry. I've got a whole lot of other stuff to eat."

"What does Ben like?" I asked Harris.

A little yellow taxi zoomed over to choose Daddy's egg salad. Harris putt-putted his cars around the salt and pepper shakers and bowls. It interested me that Harris made each of those little cars sound different.

"Are there olives with pimientos?" I asked.

"Would I forget your olives?" Daddy asked.

Mom and I chop olives into our egg salad. He turned in his chair and rummaged around in the refrigerator for them. He called to them, singing, "Knockity, knock, knock."

"Who's there?" I sang back. Harris's motor puttered to a stop as he gave me a wide-eyed look.

"Ol-live."

"Olive who?" I asked, still patting egg salad onto the bread.

"Ol-luv you." We both knock-knocked on the tops of our heads, the way we always did at the end of that joke. I probably got a little egg salad in my hair.

Out of the corner of my eye, I saw Harris tap the top of his own head.

"Olives are on the shelf in the door," I said, slapping bread on top of the sandwiches. This time I would have to eat them along with the sandwich instead of in it.

Daddy opened the jar and offered the olives to Harris, who eyed them suspiciously. "Me first," I said.

"So what are you and Ben up to?" Daddy asked me as he swung the jar in my direction. Maybe I could take my share for the whole week before Harris put his fuzzy fingers into the jar.

"Ben found something in the tide pool, and we dug a canal to let it swim back to the ocean."

Daddy gave me a curious look. "That sounds like work."

"Hard work," I said. "We're really, really tired of digging."

"Why don't you quit?"

I didn't want to tell it in a way that Harris could repeat, in case he could repeat. I couldn't say sand sharks don't bite, but I had to get the point across.

"You know those fish with fins that people are afraid of? Only some of them aren't dangerous? Some people don't know that about them. And I didn't tell. Only now some people might feel stupid if I tell."

"I see," Daddy said as I slipped the sandwiches

into a plastic bag. "So you figure you'll set it loose."

"That's what I thought. At first. Only now I'm tired of the whole idea." I got the bucket Daddy kept by the water heater and a bigger one that Mom had used to hold ice. They were cleaner than my bucket. I said, "I thought somebody else could tell."

"I hope not," Daddy said. "Somebody tells now, you lose the big moment."

"What big moment?"

"It's hard work, sure, but when you're done you have this great story. Both of you will be telling that story to each other for—well, for a long time."

I didn't think Daddy was getting it. "I thought you could tell. Like neither one of us knew about certain fish."

"He won't be fooled. Not for long," Daddy said. "You've been coming out here too long not to know about . . . fish. And he'll be mad at me too."

That was a no. My shoulders slumped. More digging.

Daddy said, "Say, maybe Harris would li—"

"Forget it," I said before Harris could get a hopeful look in his eyes. "He can't come."

"Why not?"

"Because Ben will worry about him getting eaten."

"Oh?" Daddy's eyes widened. "Oh! I get it."

I said, "So is there any other idea you can think of to help me?"

"You've already dug the canal, right?" Daddy leaned back in his chair. "The hard part's done."

"I guess."

"Just get the thing back in the ocean."

I gave up. I got two cold sodas and put them in one bucket, the other bucket held the sandwiches and a bag of chips. Salt is good when you're sweating.

I was almost out the door when Daddy said, "I have two words of advice for you, Stanley."

He meant the Stanley who went into the jungle. I forget the whole story. "Yeah?"

"Sunscreen."

So I put the sunscreen into the bucket with the sodas. I didn't want to get it all over my hands until after I ate. There's nothing worse than a sandwich that tastes like sunscreen.

When I left, Daddy was singing his version of "My Bonnie Lies over the Ocean," which Mom says he is not to sing in front of children, meaning me. Harris was motoring along to the tune.

Fourteen

While I was gone, Ben had dug the canal deeper. I could stand in the deep end of it and the edge came up to my knees, the waves rushed up around my ankles. The water was really getting rough out there, the ocean seemed kind of loud.

Ben ate both of his sandwiches and half of mine. He tried to look like he was thinking but I thought he was tired. We didn't talk much. Good beachcombing stuff would wash up by morning, that was what I thought about while I ate.

My sandwich was a little crunchy on one side from holding it with sandy fingertips. Ben's had to be crunchy pretty much all over. He was Harris's brother, all right.

When he finished eating, he said, "It must have to be really brave to live out there all alone."

"The shark?" He must have been doing some thinking after all. "Maybe not as brave as a *little* fish."

"Well, yeah," Ben said. "Not only the shark. It's so big out there, that's what I mean."

"I forgot you never saw the ocean before." Right away, I knew I shouldn't have said it. "Since you were little, I mean. It must've looked bigger then."

"I saw it in the movies," he said.

"I forgot for a minute," I said. "I never saw"— I thought fast, and I thought big—"New York City. I didn't mean anything by it."

"You've never been to New York?"

"Have you?"

"Yeah," he said. "You have to be pretty brave to live there all alone too."

I didn't say anything. I was finished eating, so I started putting on sunscreen.

"Of course, I'm not saying I was all alone."

"I knew what you meant."

"Sorry," he said.

"Me too."

I drank my whole soda, so I had to walk back to the house to use the bathroom. Daddy had moved the deck furniture down to the beach. Vicky sat at the table with Daddy, sipping iced coffee. She had her feet tucked up under her long skirt. "Did you set it free already?" she asked.

I guessed Daddy had told her. Or she'd heard me tell Daddy. "Not yet," I said. "Way not yet."

Harris puttered around them, stopping for a moment to raise his arms and make weird noises like a garbage truck or maybe a dump truck. I climbed the steps to the deck.

If this had been a usual day at the beach, Mom and Daddy would've been swimming for hours already. I'd be messing around at the edge of the water with my finds or paddling close to shore. I don't much like swimming when the water is rough, but Daddy does. His hair was still dry. It was not a usual day.

"You put on any of that sunscreen?" Daddy asked when I went back outside.

"Yep."

"Everybody gets one bad burn, right at the start of summer," Daddy said. "Better put on a little more."

So Vicky rubbed some of her suntan lotion on me, getting the spot between the shoulder blades where I could hardly reach. It felt cool and nice—not too cold, the way it does when I have a bad burn. It felt better having Vicky worry about my sunburn than thinking about old summers.

"Caught it in time, I think," she said. "We'll put a little more on when this dries on you. Arms, shoulders, and back, that's where you need it most."

I guarded while Ben walked back to use the bathroom. I rubbed in a lot more sunscreen. I rubbed it in until I couldn't soak it up anymore.

When Ben came back, he told me Daddy told him he could have just walked into the ocean. "Is that what you're going to do from now on?" I asked.

"What I'm *not* going to do," Ben said, "is follow Jim into the water." A person could get to appreciate Ben.

When we poured the first buckets of water into the pool, we saw the water level had been falling off pretty fast. The shark had been swimming in much smaller circles.

I started to feel better about this project. The water in the pool wouldn't have lasted till the tide came in. "If you didn't find this shark, it would have died out here," I said. "You saved its life."

"Thanks," he said, "for helping."

Water is heavy. That was what Ben told me to make it okay that I could only carry half a bucket's worth on my own. We tried filling my bucket to the top and sharing the carrying of it. Ben was too much taller than I was and we spilled a lot of the water.

Ben hauled both buckets by himself when I got so tired I spilled a lot of the water all by myself. He was so nice about it I sort of wished I'd told him about sand sharks. He'd gotten the water level up when Mrs. Brady walked by with her dog, Prissy, on the end of a leash.

I felt like just sitting there, but I got into position to guard.

Ben went up to her like a policeman and said, "Ma'am, I recommend you carry the canine. Sharks have been sighted in the area."

Just like that.

I dropped to my knees as Mrs. Brady hurried away.

When he came back to me, he said, "Why are you laying with your face in the sand?"

I made sure all the laughter was out of me before I rolled over. "I think it helps sunburn," I said.

"Huh. Well, when you're finished, I don't think you should stand so close to the pool like you were. The fresh seawater's made the shark feel a little peppier."

He was right about that. It was swimming faster circles. Ben made a lot more trips, hauling two buckets each time. The top part of the pool was much wider than the bottom and took more water to fill.

I lost count of how many buckets of water Ben carried. By the last trip, he had this horrible gritted-teeth look that made me afraid he would really be mad if he ever found out about sand sharks.

"Let me pour the water in," I said as he finished the last trip.

"I don't think you ought to get too close," Ben said.

"You're doing all the work and it isn't fair."

He gave in. "I'll stand next to you and warn you if he comes after you."

"Deal," I said. I hoped I would sound kind of like I was fourteen. I couldn't help grinning. I couldn't stop it the whole time I poured. I kept grinning.

"What's the matter with you?" Ben asked.

"It's the sun," I said.

He looked worried. "Sunstroke?"

I didn't know what it was. Talking about sunstroke made me feel sort of weak. I lay back in the sand and let laughter trickle out of me. I did know what it was. Ben was such a worrier. I didn't know why that seemed so funny.

Anyway, he sat down on the sand and said in this really annoyed way, "Girls." Even that didn't make me straighten up. I thought about his serious face when he'd said, *I recommend you carry the canine,* and I laughed until the whole weird feeling leaked away.

We dug some more.

Daddy and Vicky and Harris walked over to take a look at the shark. I figured Vicky wore the long skirt to hide her puffy legs. She said she felt better, though.

I worried at first that they'd do that grown-up thing of smirks and private looks. They were fine, they acted like they were touring the aquarium. Daddy held Harris in his arms as if the shark might actually be dangerous. The shark did its part and let its back fin skim the surface as it swam in circles. Harris was so impressed his motor shorted out.

I heard Ben ask Daddy how long a tunnel he thought we'd dug. "Fifty feet, easy," Daddy said.

When he and Vicky left to walk further along the shore, they warned us to be careful. Ben said, "Yes, sir," like he was in the army. And still they didn't grin at each other.

Well, Daddy looked like he might. Vicky frowned at him without even moving her eyebrows.

"I wonder what that was about," Ben said to me.

"What?"

"The death look."

"The death look?"

"When she looks at you like that, you have to toe the line," Ben said entirely seriously. "I wonder what Jim did."

I didn't know if I should be mad. Who was Ben to talk about anything my daddy did? Then again, I knew what Daddy was being warned not to do and I felt better knowing Vicky could stop him with a look.

Ben eyed the canal. He was one of those people who like to get things just so. Who think things have to be perfect. Daddy would probably get on Ben's nerves.

He might get on Vicky's nerves. I looked back at Daddy and Vicky, who were further off, and it didn't matter so much that they were laughing. They walked so they bumped into each other, the way I walked with my friends when we were having a really good time.

So he hadn't gotten on her nerves much yet.

Harris was running along the edge of the water, and Vicky swooped in to grab him and spin him around. Her skirt got really wet. I knew how the sand would be clumping up around the hem. She didn't stop to shake it off. Maybe she didn't mind. I liked that.

"Do you think that's safe?" Ben asked.

"What?"

"Walking in the surf." And then, like I'd missed something important, he added, "There are sharks in the water."

"Out where the water is deep," I reminded him. "This one got stuck here when the tide went out."

He watched them for another few seconds, then went back to digging. "Where's your dad?" I asked him.

"He lives in New York. He trades."

"What does he trade?" I said, watching Daddy put his arm around Vicky's shoulders.

"Corn and oats, stuff like that."

Before I could wonder about that, he added, "Mack's father is in Baltimore. He has a car dealership, so he's lots more reliable."

"My mom is in Baltimore too," I said.

"I know," Ben said. "Listen, do you think the tide is coming in?"

"Probably not yet," I said. "It has something to do with the moon."

"Let's dig this canal deeper," Ben said. "Then we can put more water in the pool. Maybe it will be enough to carry him out and we won't have to wait for the tide."

Fifteen

After a while Vicky and Daddy came back and helped. That is, Daddy and Ben stood the same way, each with a hand over his chin, and talked about how deep the canal needed to be. Vicky and I dug.

She acted a little helpless at first, but when I started digging, she pitched in. She didn't get annoyed about her skirt, which got pretty sandy all over.

Harris scampered back and forth in the canal. After a warning from Ben, he stayed between his mother and the water's edge, running on a new, deeper motor. He said he was a steam shovel.

He could talk if he wanted to.

"Seems to me we're doing more than our share of the work," Vicky said to me.

I stopped digging. She didn't sound too unhappy about it. Not the way Mom would have sounded. I didn't know what Vicky expected me to say. After a moment of looking at me looking at her, Vicky turned to Daddy and said cheerfully, "I think it's about time you two engineers put a little shoulder into this effort."

"All right," Daddy said. "Ben, you give a hand with the digging. I'll get some more water into the pool."

Daddy filled the pool near to overflowing, making about ten trips. He did it a lot faster than Ben could. Of course, he was bigger and stronger than Ben, which counted for a lot. And he hadn't done any digging.

The water seeped through the sand that still kept the tide pool dammed up. "It won't hold much longer," Ben told us.

"You're ready to give it a try, anyway," Daddy said.

The sand shark had been swimming more rapidly around and around since Daddy had added the fresh cold water to the pool. The shark looked like it was getting ready too, making a sudden turn into a figure eight, or giving its tail an extra little flip now and then.

Vicky took Harris by the hand and stood back from the pool. Daddy took up a position halfway between the tide pool and the sea. He held an extra bucket of water to help wash the shark along in case it got stuck on the way.

"You keep an eye on the shark," Ben told me. "Let me know if he looks like he's going to go for me."

"Right," I said. I was too tired to find this even a little bit funny.

Ben dropped to his knees, and chopped at the sand with the bucket. The dam broke. Water gushed into the canal.

Ben fell backward for safety, but the shark acted like it had been given a set of instructions. It skimmed the surface of the water, racing for the sea. Daddy poured the extra bucket of water into the canal as the shark rushed past him.

I ran a little ways, hoping to keep up as the shark raced the water to the sea. A few seconds later, it was gone.

"Well," Ben said. He'd come to stand near Daddy, his hands on his hips. He sounded a little disappointed that things had gone so well.

"This deserves a celebration," Daddy said.

"Celebration?" Ben echoed.

He missed that shark, I could tell. He missed the shark or maybe the feeling he'd had before he set it free. Like it was a moment to save in his memory. I could have told him it would be like that, but he wouldn't have believed me.

I hoped he would look my way, that he would have something to say to me. I hoped we would have a story to tell each other later, the way Daddy said.

"Hamburgers on the grill and all the marshmallows we can eat," Daddy said.

"Yea-ay," Harris crowed.

Vicky said, "You guys make a great shark rescue team. I never saw anything like it."

And Ben gave me a big grin.

Sixteen

Vicky made dinner. That is, she put the burgers on the grill and went back inside to make a salad. Daddy put on a CD and danced around the deck, singing along. Sometimes he stopped singing to say things like "Wonder what that shark is telling all his friends?"

Once he threw his fist in the air and yelled, "Sharkbusters!" loudly enough that they heard it on the deck next door. Over the sound of the ocean.

Everybody waved.

I entertained Harris. He sat next to me while I spread out all the stuff in my bucket to dry on the deck. There were mostly shells and bottles, a couple of pieces of pale green glass rubbed smooth. He had to touch everything. I didn't mind. Stuff that comes out of the ocean has its own furriness.

Ben watched us for a while, then went inside and came back with his earphones on. He sat on one of the steps down low. I figured he had to sit there to get away from Daddy's music.

Harris wanted to look at the stuff I keep on the bookshelves in the kitchen, my collection. He brought out a couple of the pieces of tangled fishing line, which are always my favorites. I took them away from him and carried them back in.

That they're tangled is what makes them so good. One of them is wound tight around a piece of sea glass. When we hang it in a window and the sun shines through, it showers the room with blue dots of light.

Vicky didn't see me put them back. She was busy making a salad.

Then Harris brought out the horseshoe crab I'd found last summer. Daddy let me keep it because it had been dead a long time and only smelled a little bit. It was my favorite too.

The tail broke when Harris used it for a handle.

Vicky caught up with Harris in time to see the pieces fall on the deck. He yelled and Daddy hurried over to help. Vicky bumped heads with Daddy, grabbing to be the one to pick it up. "Ow!"

Harris dropped the horseshoe crab tail and it broke.

He stood like a statue.

I knew Harris was sure he was going to get yelled at. I wanted to yell at him. But I said, "I guess it was getting pretty old." I still had all the parts, after all.

Ben stood up, and although we couldn't see him before, I could see him now, watching to see how things were going to go. I felt a little lump in my throat, from embarrassment, but also sort of being afraid that he'd think I wasn't being nice to Harris.

Vicky told Harris he couldn't take anything else off that shelf. She didn't say it like she thought I was being selfish. She knew some stuff was mine and that's all.

Harris's face was red and a little sad, like I'd seen before. "You could bring out one of my picture books," I told him. "They're on the shelf right below. There's a beach book for every summer I've come here."

"How about that, Mack?" Vicky asked him. "We'll read one before bed."

He nodded, going indoors with her. Probably he thought "before bed" meant anytime starting now. I picked up the pieces of the horseshoe crab.

Maybe. the broken tail could be glued together. I could set it back on the shelf with the tail partway inside the shell so it would look fine.

Daddy said, "Maybe that's one to toss."

"No," I said. "It's part of my collection."

On her way back into the house, Vicky asked Daddy if he was keeping an eye on the meat. He hurried over to turn the hamburgers.

"Hope everybody likes them well done," he called inside to her.

Vicky came out holding a towel and said, "Does that mean you haven't been watching? I should have put Ben in charge." She scratched her leg.

"Probably true," Daddy said, and got Vicky to dance around the deck with him in these big sweeping circles. I don't think she was mad at him to start with but dancing made her all smiles. She flipped the towel around like it was something fancy.

Ben looked sort of disgusted with them. He had looked that way once or twice before when they acted romantic.

It did feel weird to see Daddy doing all the things that got on Mom's nerves and then see Vicky make it okay. Or just let it be okay. I don't know which. Sometimes when Mom got mad, Daddy would say this or that didn't *used* to get on her nerves.

Harris came back outside with three books. He sat down close to me and started to look at the pictures in one of them. I put some bottles back into my bucket to be cleaned up later.

When Daddy and Vicky took the burgers off the grill, Vicky was the one who put them on a plate. Daddy sort of hung around her, holding the plate and looking at her in a way that made Vicky blush.

Ben seemed embarrassed by the whole thing. When he took the chair at the end of the table, he said, "We'll let you two teenagers sit together."

I expected Daddy to say something, like Ben wasn't in charge of where people sat. Or that Vicky would shoot Ben the death look. But Daddy played along and slid into the chair next to Vicky.

Vicky laughed in this flirty way and said, "Harris, come to the table, honey."

So he did. He climbed onto the other end chair and gave me what I'd come to think of as his big boy smile, lots of teeth showing. I was glad my chair was right in the middle. And I gave him a bigger big boy smile right back.

That made him look down at his plate and— I don't know why—made me feel a little ashamed of myself. Okay, he'd broken my horseshoe crab, but I knew he didn't mean to.

Vicky was complaining about new flea bites on her ankle, so I don't think she saw anything. Neither did Ben. "These burgers aren't as done as they looked," he said as red juice trickled down his wrist.

After the first bite, he ate without talking. We all did. Harris could keep his motor going while he chewed, but now he was mostly quiet. Saving sharks was hungry work.

We were almost done before Daddy tried out

one of his riddles. "How do you know an elephant's been in your kitchen?" Daddy asked.

Ben answered, "His footprints are in the peanut butter," as if he was bored.

"Ow," Daddy said. "Got me."

Ben rolled his eyes and said, "That's the one you told me the first time you took Mom out."

"I never heard that one before," I said. I never knew Daddy told riddles for anyone else either. It was kind of a sickening thing to find out.

"Knock, knock," Daddy said, looking at me.

I decided to get over it. Otherwise Ben might think I was a baby after all. I said, "Who's there?"

"Wendy."

"Wendy who?"

Daddy said, "Wendy phone rings, answer it."

Harris laughed. Really laughed. Ben looked at me like *What a baby,* so I didn't dare laugh. I didn't think this was fair. Just because Ben was mad, it didn't mean I had to be mad. But it wasn't the right time to say so. Besides, if I was going to be mad, we might be mad about different things.

Harris laughed enough for both of us. Daddy asked Harris, "What was Tigger doing in the outhouse?"

"Bathroom," Ben said in a rude way.

"Ben," Vicky said.

He said, "Harris doesn't know what an outhouse is. He's a little kid," making Harris look down at his plate again. I'd only known Harris for a day but I knew he didn't like it when somebody made being a little kid the same thing as being stupid. I didn't like it either.

"Okay, okay," Daddy said. "What was Tigger doing in the bathroom?"

Harris was still looking at his plate.

"Looking for Pooh!" Daddy shouted like everyone was having a good time, and Harris squeezed his eyes shut and laughed this loud fake laugh.

"More potato salad?" Vicky asked, offering the container to Daddy.

Seventeen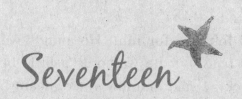

Daddy told her he'd never really liked potato salad from the deli. Ben got a funny look in his eye and told Daddy it wasn't from the deli. His mom made it herself.

"We didn't get this at the store?" Daddy said, looking innocent.

"I brought it from home," Vicky said. "I use the containers over again."

So Daddy said he was sorry about the potato salad. He really liked the fruit salad with the marshmallows in it. Vicky said that was from the deli. And Ben pushed the bowl across to him, saying, "Here, have another helping, dude."

"Ben." This went with Vicky's death look.

So nobody else saw how sad Harris still looked.

I felt bad for him. His hands were furry, it was true, but he was only a little boy. "Knock, knock," I said in a low voice meant for Harris.

"Who's there?" he whispered without looking at me.

"Wuv."

"Wuv who?"

I said, "I wuv you."

He looked at me, the corners of his mouth turning up. Then looked quickly down again. I could tell he felt better.

"I wuv you too," Vicky said, and gave him a hand hug.

Vicky reached across the table and squeezed my hand too. It was weird, but I didn't mind that it was the same hand that touched Harris's furry hand. Especially considering he wasn't just furry but had potato salad between his fingers now too. I waited a little bit before I used my napkin.

"Here, I've got one," Daddy was saying. "What's lumpy and brown and has X-ray vision?"

"Are these glows-in-the-dark jokes?" Ben said

in a way that made it clear he wouldn't think that was very funny.

I felt better suddenly, knowing this was one of Daddy's made-up jokes, and knowing that Ben didn't know that. Daddy was fighting back in his own way, and I was glad. I didn't like when Ben said things that made everybody feel uncomfortable.

Daddy asked again, "What's lumpy and brown and has X-ray vision?" and then gave Harris the punch line to the joke. "A baked potato."

Harris laughed. Really laughed, like the first time.

"I don't get it," Ben said, but not in the rude voice he'd been using.

Harris laughed harder. "Poe-tay—ha, ha, ha—toes," he said, "have—eyes."

"Har-ris," Vicky said like she could hardly believe he got it. She was beginning to laugh too.

Daddy loves to tell his vegetable jokes. "What's purple, has a tail, and goes 'bzzzzzzzz'?"

Laughter seemed to burst out of Harris, and he hadn't heard the end of the joke.

"A beet, when you plug it in," Daddy sang out happily. He loves when somebody appreciates his jokes. Ben looked at Daddy like he'd lost his mind.

For some reason that struck *me* funny and I laughed too.

"What's green and sings 'It's a Small World' when you plug it in?"

Harris laughed all the more. He could hardly stay on his chair.

"Electric lettuce," I said loudly, to be heard over Harris.

Harris screamed with laughter.

"Stop, stop," Vicky yelled. She was still laughing. She leaned across the corner of the table, trying to hold Harris up. "I demand to know what you've put in the food. Silly stuff."

"Haaaa, silly, haa, ha, stuff!" Harris yelled. His face went dark red.

"Harris, settle down. Mack," Vicky said, shaking him a little. "I'm afraid you're going to make yourself sick."

"Nope," he told her. Another laugh burst out of him.

"He's overtired," Vicky said to Daddy. "He gets like this when he's missed his nap."

"I don't mind when he's like this," Daddy said.

"You've got potato salad on your sleeve," Ben said to Vicky in such a mean voice Harris stopped laughing. I didn't know why a little potato salad would upset someone who didn't care that his brother's hands were furry. Whose hands might once have been furry too.

My mind went right past the surprise of it to understanding that he'd gotten upset about Vicky and Daddy. He'd been mad since they danced on the deck.

"Ben, we're all going to quiet down now," Vicky said, giving him what was definitely a death look. "So nothing is going to slip by me. Change your attitude right now."

It was Ben's turn to look down at his plate. After a long moment of everyone being too quiet, Harris looked at Daddy and said, "Tell some more."

"After dinner, maybe," Daddy said, going along with Vicky. He was pleased to have Harris thinking he was so funny, but he didn't push it.

"I'm still itching," Vicky said, rubbing her legs.

Daddy said, "Put some more calamine lotion on."

"Sometimes it takes a while to get over flea bites," I told her. "It took Mom a whole month once."

Vicky scratched again and Daddy looked sort of disappointed. When I looked in Ben's direction, he smiled at me. A real smile. The thing I found myself thinking, Ben didn't want to be coming here on weekends.

That gave me a funny feeling in the bottom of my stomach.

Because as much as I didn't want them coming here either, it had been fun to set the shark free. Vicky was nice enough to care that the horseshoe crab was important to me. I even liked the little truck sounds Harris was making as he picked his hamburger apart.

I didn't like it that Ben didn't feel the same way about Daddy and me.

Eighteen

After dinner, Daddy cleared the table. "I'll do the dishes," he said.

I couldn't remember a time when Daddy had said he'd do the dishes. I looked out at the water instead of at him. A couple of bonfires had been started a little distance along the beach while we were eating.

The sun was going down and I was glad. I tried to imagine the people making bonfires were the same people who made bonfires every year, but probably they weren't. They might even be people who'd never come to the shore before. They didn't even know the tide was coming in.

Vicky put marshmallows on the ends of the barbecue forks and told Ben and me to roast them over the glowing coals in the grill. "Don't get too close," she said. "And don't let them get too black. We're having s'mores for dessert."

"S'mores?" Harris asked.

Vicky said, "They're called that because you always want some more."

"We're going to hear about Mom's Girl Scout days now," Ben said with a smirk.

Vicky quickly made an okay sign and flicked him on the head with her finger. Hard.

"Ow!"

"Don't be obnoxious," she said. "You won't get any dessert."

"All right, all right," he said. "Some people can't take a joke."

"Keep in mind you aren't the only one who can get funny," Vicky said as she went back inside.

"What we do," Ben told Harris, as if he and his mom had not been arguing, "we make them into a sandwich with graham crackers and Hershey's bars." Ben could be mad one minute and act like he didn't know it the next. It was a good thing about him.

Vicky came back out with a handful of Hershey's bars. "Mack, I'd like you to open up these chocolate bars for dessert." She put them in front of him. "Put them on this plate."

He picked one up in his furry little hands and turned it over, looking for the glued-together place. I could feel my eyes go wide. I didn't mind him touching my shells but I didn't want him to touch my food.

On her way back inside, Vicky looked over her shoulder and said, "No bites." My breath got stuck in my throat.

"Hey," Ben said, nudging my elbow with his. "Don't let your marshmallows get so close to the fire. They'll get flamed."

"Aren't they brown enough yet?" I asked. I wanted to be done. I wanted to get my Hershey's bar away from Harris.

"You want them to melt on the inside," he said. Then he yelled, "Graham crackers needed out here."

I couldn't keep my eyes off Harris. Daddy stepped out with the package of graham crackers and stepped back inside before I could signal him with a look.

"Quit jiggling," Ben said. "The marshmallows will fall off if they're soft." And right then one of his did. The smell of burnt sugar sweetened the air.

Vicky checked our marshmallows and said, "Okay, those are ready." She quickly spread the crackers out on the tablecloth. Then she took one of Ben's forks and squished the marshmallow onto the graham crackers.

I jiggled mine again. Not one marshmallow hung like it might fall off. Harris started on the third chocolate bar. When he got it out of the paper, he held it to his nose and sniffed it. He licked it a little bit. I wanted to scream. All that came out was a tiny squeak.

Ben looked at me in this sharp way that reminded me of Vicky, and I jiggled my marshmallows. "I might like to have mine without chocolate," I said.

"Oh, no, you wouldn't," Vicky said, sounding very happy with herself. "Without the chocolate, it's just crackers and marshmallow."

Vicky took Ben's second fork. "I think mine are readier," I said.

Vicky said, "Hold still so they don't fall off."

144

Ben strolled over to watch Harris put the next-to-last chocolate bar on the plate. Ben reached down and swept the last chocolate bar up, saying, "This one is Lexie's."

Harris looked up like he thought there would be more instructions.

Ben said, "I think she can open it herself."

I expected Harris to fuss but he didn't. He nodded and motored away. He had a fire truck waiting for him at the end of the deck. I thought the trunk of their car must have been full of toy trucks. Vicky put out a different one every couple of hours.

She took one of my forks so I had a hand free when Ben offered me the chocolate bar. "Thanks," I said. I didn't look at him. I made my s'more. Vicky put Ben in charge of making one for Harris, and Vicky made Daddy's.

Most cookies and crackers go all soft in a by-the-ocean way after a while but the graham cracker was still crisp. The marshmallows were sweet and sticky. The chocolate melted a little. Perfect.

I moved to the edge of the deck to eat it.

Ben came to sit on the top step with his

s'more and we watched the water lap over the bottom steps. We watched the sky and the sea go black while we stretched out our dessert for as long as we could and licked our fingers. We did want some more.

When I finished, I wrapped my arms around my legs and rested my chin on my knees. My skin felt tight and sore and, on my back, too hot. The tide had come in, so the water sloshed around under the house. I felt a little sleepy.

Because Vicky had taken some more of the allergy medicine after dinner, she fell asleep in a deck chair in about five minutes. Nobody minded really, we were all so tired.

Except Daddy, I suppose. He still cared. He sang a little song or two, pretending to strum a guitar. Vicky didn't wake up to listen and it wasn't very long before Harris crawled up in the deck chair beside her.

"The ocean. It's big, and it's dark," Ben said.

The tide put out the bonfires on the beach. I guessed Ben was thinking about the shark, out there all alone. "It's their home," I said. "They like it there."

He didn't say anything to that.

"Thanks again for saving the chocolate," I said, because I hadn't really said it the right way before. Saying it in mostly darkness felt better.

"It's okay," he said. "I know how you feel."

I could see his face well enough in the moonlight. "Why didn't you rescue your own chocolate?"

"Oh, I don't care," he said. "You get used to it when he's around all the time."

I doubted that. I asked, "What do you mean, then, that you know how I feel?"

"Don't get me wrong," Ben said in a low voice. "Your dad's a real nice guy and it's great that he wants us to have fun and all. . . ."

I had an idea I knew. "It's that he can be so silly," I said.

"Huh?" Ben said. "No, see, that's what I was afraid of, you think I've got a problem with Jim."

"You don't mind when he acts like a kid?"

"Of course not," Ben said. "He's just having fun."

"So what bothers you?"

"Well, my mom," he said in an annoyed way.

"What's Vicky done?"

"It's the way she's acting," he said. He lowered his voice again to say, "All girly. Because Jim's around."

"Yep," I said. "She's acting silly."

Ben pounced on that. "See, you saw it too."

"I thought she was having fun," I said. Ben looked at me like I'd said something mean. His mother called him to help Daddy in the kitchen. He didn't move.

I asked him, "How come it's silly when your mom acts like that and it isn't so silly when Daddy acts like that?"

"I don't know." Ben looked away. "It's just the way it is."

I put my chin back on my knees. "I know what you mean."

Nineteen

I hadn't called my mom. By then Vicky was awake and sitting with Harris in the kitchen. She was reading one of my beach books to him. He kept laughing his funny deep laugh.

A few minutes later, she took him off to bed. I still couldn't call. Daddy was hunting around for something in the kitchen and he might say something to Vicky. And Mom would wonder, "Who else is there?"

I got this idea to give everyone time to fall asleep and then I could use the phone. It wouldn't be all that late and I could say I didn't want to interrupt her favorite show. Ha-ha.

So I got ready for bed, like everybody else. And the next thing I knew, it was morning. Somebody was up, making kitchen noises. There was sand in my bed, I felt it when I moved my foot.

I'd fallen asleep before I finished buttoning my pajama top, worrying I wasn't going to be able to lie down on my sunburn. I spent the whole night at the wrong end of the bed.

I woke up thinking Mom probably thought I was having such a good time that I didn't think about her at all, when really I hadn't even gone swimming yet. Worse, it made me sad to think of her waiting for me to call.

I'd watch for everybody to go out and then I would call. And I would find something really special on the shore and take it home to her.

At the table, Harris sat in the chair next to Vicky's, although she was still in the bathroom. Daddy hadn't come to the table yet either. He was making breakfast.

"What would you like, Harris, me boy?" Daddy said in his leprechaun voice. "We have bacon or sausage, toast, and scrambled."

Harris looked confused.

"He means we're eating eggs," I said to Harris. I tipped my plate so he could look at what I was eating. "This is scrambled, see? Do you want bacon or sausage?"

Harris made the rumbling sound of a truck starting up.

"Could you put that to me in English, please?" Daddy asked Harris.

While Daddy tried to talk to Harris, Ben brought a computer magazine to the table and began to read. Just the sight of him with that magazine made my stomach go all tight. I couldn't say why.

Harris pretty much pretended he didn't know Daddy was talking to him. He ran a little pink Volkswagen around the sugar bowl and between the salt and pepper shakers. "Harris?"

"Harris wants you to call him Mack," Ben said from behind his magazine.

I waited to see what Daddy would say. When I was real little, like Harris, I tried to get Daddy to call me Simba and let me call him Pumbaa. Mom would do it. She called me Simba and I called her Timon all the time.

When I called Daddy Pumbaa, he did what

Harris was doing, he pretended not to hear me. Then he would say, "I think it's really important for people to be themselves."

Mom would say, "She's three. This is who she is at three."

Daddy said, "I wouldn't mind if she was Simba for an afternoon. I mind that she's Simba all the time. I want her to know it's okay with me if she's Lexie."

I did it for a year, I think Mom said. I nearly forgot what my name really was, that was how long I did it. Daddy would never play along, he always ruined it.

"He won't answer to anything but Mack," Ben said. He still hadn't come out from behind the magazine.

Daddy said, "I've been calling him Harris."

"Yeah, you can call him anything you want to. I don't mean this to be rude, but he only answers to Mack." Ben folded the magazine down toward his face for a moment. "And right now, you want an answer."

"Mack," Daddy said. "I need to know what you're eating for breakfast."

Harris stood up on his chair and motored the

pink Volkswagen over to my plate, backfired, and zipped away. Harris was almost as good as a cartoon. "Ben?" Daddy said.

Ben sighed and put his magazine down. "French toast?" Ben asked Harris. Daddy probably didn't know how to make french toast, but Harris's motor muttered down.

"Eggs Benedict," Ben said in the same way he says, "Deal."

"Cereal, then," Daddy said, ignoring Ben. "We have Corn Chex and Cheerios."

Harris appeared to brighten up. "Va vroom."

"Cold eggs," Ben said, picking up the magazine again. "He wants cold eggs."

Daddy looked at me, probably because he couldn't see Ben.

I shrugged.

"I brought hard-boiled eggs," Vicky called from the bathroom.

"I used them up for the egg salad yesterday," Daddy said. "But it's easy enough, I guess."

He reached for a pot and started to run water into it.

I saw a look flicker over Ben's face, but then he went back to reading his magazine. Harris's motor made sounds like a truck stuck in the mud.

Daddy put three eggs into the water. Harris's motor got louder.

When Daddy turned on the stove, Harris whined, "Don't cook it."

"Ben?" Vicky called from the bathroom. "Are you helping?"

From behind the magazine, Ben said, "He won't eat a hot hard-boiled egg. And he doesn't get it about cooking it."

Daddy lost his place for a moment, but then he had an idea. He put a bowl and another egg in front of Harris. "Feel how cold that egg is?"

Harris put a hand on the egg reluctantly.

"Open that egg into the bowl," Daddy told him.

Harris shook his head a little. Mainly it was the motor sound that said no. So Daddy reached over and broke the egg.

He was quick, too quick for Harris, who saw what Daddy was about to do and reached to stop him. "No!" Harris yelled, but it was too late.

The egg was broken into the bowl. And Harris started to wail.

Ben said, "It's ruined."

"It's not ruined," Daddy said loudly so Harris would hear him. "It's not even cooked."

"He doesn't get it," Ben said without looking up.

"What?" Daddy yelled, because Harris was really belting it out now.

"He doesn't get it!" Ben yelled back.

Vicky came in then, saying, "My fault, my fault. Should have gotten up to shower before everybody else was up."

Seeing Vicky calmed Harris down. He cried more quietly. It was like now that his mother was here, he had hopes of getting some cold eggs to eat.

"Don't be silly," Daddy said in his usual voice, since Harris had quieted down. "It's your vacation too. Why should you have to get up at the crack of dawn?"

"So breakfast will be peaceful, that's why," Vicky said. She sounded almost cheerful. Harris stopped crying. "Don't we have a little of that egg salad left over from yesterday?"

Ben got up from the table.

"Have you had breakfast, Ben?" Vicky asked.

"I'm going to the bathroom," he said.

Harris accepted an egg salad sandwich made with half a slice of bread. Daddy sat down to eat while Vicky made more toast to go around and sat down.

Ben hadn't come back to the table.

We heard the door close when he went into the bathroom but we didn't hear him sneak out.

Twenty

"Do you want to look for him?" Daddy asked Vicky.

"No," Vicky said in a voice that wasn't cheerful anymore. "It's not like he ran away or something. He's gone off by himself. He'll be back when he gets hungry."

"Well, it's good he didn't eat much, then," Daddy said. He was being careful not to look at Harris, who had egg salad between his fingers and at the corners of his mouth. Harris was a mess.

"I'm going out too," I said.

I wanted to call Mom. Except for when I didn't want to. There was too much happening to talk to her. Besides, if Ben and Harris kept giving Daddy a hard time, maybe the weekends would be just Daddy and me.

Daddy said to me, "Why don't you stick around?"

I stood half out of my chair. He'd never said I couldn't go beachcombing. Ever.

Harris slid out of his chair, motor revving, and ran, heading for the bedrooms. Vicky chased after him, saying, "Harris. Mack. Don't touch anything, okay?"

"Maybe you could think of me as a sand shark," Daddy said. "Stick around and help me out."

I shrugged. What was I supposed to do?

In the bathroom, Vicky said, "Hold still, won't you? The cloth isn't even wet." Mack rumbled at her.

Daddy said, "Since we got here, you're always on your way out to do something."

I sat back down. "You can come beachcombing," I said, and probably I sounded a lot like Mary Tyler Moore.

I wanted to be by myself after wanting to be with Daddy all weekend. It's funny how that happens sometimes, that I need to be by myself for a few minutes or I get crabby. Mom always sees it coming, she says, and now sometimes I do too.

"Not right now, I can't," he said, and I got this little sick feeling. Even though I wanted to go by myself.

Harris raced through the kitchen to the back deck, vrrrrrrrrmmm. Vicky went through at a walk, still carrying a washcloth. I felt a lot like Harris. I had to run around until I felt better.

"Relationships are work," Daddy said, leaning toward me. "I need a little help here."

"If somebody helps now, you could miss your big moment," I said.

I tried to say it nicely, because really I didn't mean it any other way. It was the only thing I could think of to say.

I felt sort of bad but mainly I wanted to go outside. "I'm sorry."

"No. No, I'm having another cup of coffee and doing the dishes," he said.

I helped him carry the dishes to the sink. "Go on," he said. "Things will be okay here."

Because it made me nervous that we didn't know where Ben had gone, I said, "I'm going the other way today." I wanted Daddy to know where he could find me.

"Whaddya think, Stanley?" Daddy asked.

"Sunscreen," I said. I went to the bathroom to put it on. My sunburn felt a lot better this morning. Ben's toothbrush was in the sink. Horrible.

Outside, it was already getting hot. There were kids running around, people sitting out on towels. And the water looked calm. People were going swimming.

I'd left my bucket on the steps and it wasn't there now. I looked for it under the house, hoping it hadn't gotten washed away by the tide. Ben was standing under the deck, in stripes of sunlight.

I walked over there. He was striped and now so was I. "Your mom is looking for you," I said in a loud whisper.

He made a motion with his hand that kind of shushed me and told me to go away at the same time. So I did. Yesterday this would have hurt my feelings. Yesterday I felt sure he didn't want to walk with me because he thought I was a little kid. Today I knew he just felt like being alone.

I saw that the tide had washed my bucket up

behind the house. When I went to get it, I saw the car and was reminded of Daddy's cell phone. I felt a whole lot better all of a sudden. I could call Mom.

Since the time Daddy went into the water with his phone in the pocket of his shorts, the rule has been no cell phone at the beach. I found it in the glove compartment.

When I flipped it open and pressed Power, nothing happened. Daddy hadn't recharged the battery. For a second I got really mad at him. Then I remembered he didn't know I was going to want to use it. I put it back in the glove compartment and started for the beach.

I didn't get to call Mom and I'd had a terrible thought. What if she called here and Vicky picked up the phone? I hoped Mom was out to breakfast with George this morning. But sometime today I had to call.

I could feel a frown on my face, sort of pinching. I'd had a few minutes to be by myself and I was still crabby. Ben was still standing there in the shade of the deck. He looked like somebody waiting for a bus. I acted like I didn't see him, the way he wanted me to.

He walked over to me. "I'm tired of being company, that's all."

"It's okay," I told him. "I'm tired of having company." I kept on going.

I didn't know what it was like to come to the beach not knowing how to swim, worried that I couldn't go into the water without being attacked by sharks. I doubted I would think it was a fun place, even if my mother wasn't acting like Mary Tyler Moore. Because right at the moment, I didn't think it was such a fun place anyway.

I hadn't gotten ten steps away from the house before I heard Vicky calling me. I turned around with a new bad feeling coming over me. "What?"

"Ben didn't happen to tell you where he was going?"

I looked at Ben. He stepped into the darker shadows under the house. I looked up at Vicky. "He's probably really close by. There's only the shore and the marsh." I couldn't see Harris, but I knew he was up there. I could hear his motor.

Vicky looked along the shore, probably hoping to see Ben. I looked at Ben, wondering why I had lied for him. I felt my forehead for a fever.

Daddy says people with a fever can do things and not know why. My forehead felt kind of hot. I hoped it was the sunburn.

Vicky turned back to me. That bad feeling got stronger. "Can Harris come with you, Lexie?" I knew she would ask that.

It wasn't that he had sticky hands and sounded like a truck. The thing that came to my mind right off, he was much littler than me and I didn't want to play babysitter.

I looked at Ben, or at the shape that was Ben. When he didn't want to explore the shore with me because I was too little, I didn't like it. More than that, I didn't like being Ben.

"He has to stay out of the water so he won't drown," I said. I still didn't want to take him. "Anything he picks up is mine if I want it. I'm beachcombing out here."

"Lexie," Daddy said, coming out of the house to stand beside Vicky. He sounded unhappy with me.

I didn't care.

He didn't tell me we were having company until we got to the shore. We weren't having our time together the way I thought we would. I was taking Harris with me.

And now Daddy wanted to act like he had complaints about *me*.

I was feeling brave, I guess. Or mad. Things were not working out the way they were supposed to and I was tired of it. I was tired of pretending I didn't mind.

I tried to give Daddy the death look. "This is my vacation too. This is my beachcombing trip and I don't have to take him with me."

I could feel my knees knock together. Actually knock. But somebody had to stand up for me and I guess it had to be me.

"You hear that?" Vicky said, looking down at Harris.

His engine revved.

"Lexie has rules, and you have to abide by them."

His engine revved again agreeably.

"All right, then. You can go."

He was something to see as he came down the steps. He had blue paint on his nose and cheeks and shoulders, and on the tops of his bare feet. Well, not paint. Some kind of sunscreen. My sitter has some in Pepto-Bismol pink.

"He needs a bucket or something," I said.

Vicky dashed inside, and by the time Harris reached the sand, she was throwing a plastic bag over the side of the deck. It didn't float on the breeze. It dropped straight down. Harris picked it up and looked inside. He pulled out a carrot.

"So it won't blow away," Vicky said. For somebody who sounded so much like Mary Tyler Moore, Vicky was pretty smart.

Harris dropped the carrot back into the bag. I showed him where I'd found the horseshoe crab's shell, right in front of the next-door deck.

Further down the shore we saw Mrs. Brady walking her pink poodle. When he barked at us, we wiggled our butts to bother him more. I always did that when I was little like Harris, and he thought it was pretty funny.

There were a lot of people outside today. People getting there for their first day at the shore, people leaning on deck rails and eating bagels. Hanging out damp blankets to dry in the sun.

We walked over a clam bed and I told Harris about putting his toes over the holes. Thoop,

thoop, thoop. He did it and stood there for a moment. Then he smiled at me, the sweetest smile, and said, "Clam kisses."

I don't know what happened, but all at once I really liked Harris. "So you like people to call you Mack, huh?"

"I'm the biggest," he said.

"I guess so," I agreed, and put my toes over as many holes as I could stretch them to reach. I'd call him Mack if that was what he wanted. I didn't think he'd forget his name was Harris, and if he did, there were people who would remind him.

Mack's motor started and he ran off along the shore. I stopped counting clam kisses and stayed close enough to save him if he ran into the water.

I had almost forgotten I'd come out here to look for sea treasure. Mack found the first piece. Squatting beside it to look it over, he didn't touch it.

"It's a sand dollar," I said. "It's the first one I've ever seen. Washed up, I mean. Dead."

"My parakeet's dead too," Mack said.

"That's sad," I said. "When did it die?"

"Yesterday." He thought this over. "A long yesterday ago."

"Oh. Well, I'm very sorry."

"We buried it in the backyard."

A little breeze blew and the stink of dead fish lifted into the air. I still had my shovel in my bucket. "We could bury this sand dollar if you want."

So we did. I dug around and under the sand dollar until it lay a little deeper in the sand. I gave the shovel to Mack. "You can help me cover it up." I used my hands to scoop up the sand I'd dug out.

At first he worked without talking to me, just kept his motor running. But when we had finished the job and I was deciding if we were supposed to say a prayer or something, Mack said, "Ben says we're getting married."

"Who are you getting married to?" I asked.

"Your daddy."

I felt really stupid. Of course it would be Daddy. Vicky wouldn't be spending the week here if she was marrying somebody else.

"I didn't know that," I said.

"I didn't know it either," Mack said.

He didn't look any happier to have found out about it than I was. In fact, he looked like a little kid whose parakeet had died. I knew how he felt.

After a moment I took his hand. It was crusted with sand. So was mine.

Twenty-One

On the way home, Mack combed the shore. Now and then he wanted me to look at something, and he put some stuff in his bag with the carrot and he put a couple of good things in my bucket. But I might as well have been walking through a fog.

Who was going to tell my mother?

It would have to be Daddy. What if he didn't tell her before I went back to Baltimore? I didn't want to know this if Mom didn't.

Maybe I could pretend not to know it. Maybe I could pretend to come down with something that gave me such a high fever I got delirious.

The good thing about pretending is sometimes it feels true.

What worried me about that was if I got delirious, maybe I would accidentally tell her. Just thinking about it made me feel sick and dizzy.

I couldn't stop thinking. I imagined Vicky would move her boys into Daddy's tiny apartment. Daddy couldn't give them my bedroom, which is really a corner next to his desk. Two boys could sleep there only if they hung from their heels like bats.

Then I realized Daddy would probably move in with them, wherever they lived. Vicky probably wouldn't have a bedroom for me. And when I had to sleep in a closet, it wouldn't even be my closet.

And out here at the beach, when I came for the weekend, Ben wouldn't be company. I would.

Vicky would be my stepmother. I thought about Vicky giving me the death look. I couldn't help it. Actually, they didn't seem so terrible, those looks, but then, she had only looked them at Ben and Daddy. I might feel differently if she looked a death look at me.

Ben and Mack would be my brothers.

Stepbrothers, but what difference would it

make? I have three friends with older steps and one friend with a younger step and nobody ever says, *Oh, this is my stepbrother.*

No.

At first they might say, *That's my new brother.* Sooner or later, they get tired of explaining their whole family. Mostly sooner, what they say is *That's my brother.*

Then that person with the ponytuft or the person with furry hands is related to them in everybody's mind. I looked at Mack, who trudged through the sand a couple of steps ahead of me.

He dragged his sack with the carrot and a few small pieces of car-shaped driftwood. The blue sunscreen had mostly worn off and his face was too pink. His hair flipped up at the front when a breeze blew, which made him look strong and brave, the way a sailboat can look when it heads into the wind.

"We're almost home," he said to me as we neared the house. He started his motor up and sped off to show Vicky all his finds.

Home. Mack called it home. Like he'd already lived with us forever.

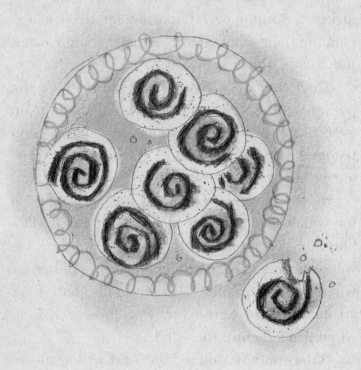

Twenty-Two

By the time I climbed the steps, Mack was laying out his finds.

Ben was back. If he was in trouble with Vicky, it didn't show. She was sitting in the sun on a deck chair and having iced tea. Ben was eating from a plate full of some of these rolled-up cookies they'd brought with them that taste kind of like apple pie. I think Ben was eating them for breakfast.

Daddy had been swimming. His hair was still wet and stood up in little spikes. But I'd had worries all morning and I didn't really care if he was having fun.

"You look like you're a million miles away, Lexie," Vicky said. "What are you thinking about?"

My mind was kind of a blank before she asked that, so maybe that was why I said, "I'm thinking about getting married." What I meant was, I was thinking about them getting married. It was too late to take it back. Vicky had been about to take a sip of her iced tea. Now she held it a few inches from her lips.

Daddy had been admiring Mack's stuff, but he stopped to look at me hard. Like I was in trouble. And we hadn't been having the best day already.

Ben was drinking soda. He snorted and it spurted right out of his nose.

"Ow, ow, that burns," he yelled.

Mack was the worst. He didn't get that I had repeated what he'd told me. He looked at me sadly, like he thought I'd had a secret I hadn't told him. Once Ben stopped yelling, Mack asked, "Is everybody getting married?"

Daddy tried to act like the whole thing was a big joke. "This sounds pretty serious," he said. He winked this big fake wink, looking at Vicky. "I think I ought to at least meet the fellow before you start thinking about marrying him, Lexie."

I felt myself go hot all over. There was probably nothing Daddy could have said that would have been right. But there was nothing he could have said that would have been more wrong.

The plate of cookies was right in front of me. I reached out and hit the edge of it so cookies flew up into the air and fell all around. "You didn't tell me you asked company to come for the week," I said. "You didn't tell me you're marrying Vicky either. You always told me it's the same thing as a lie if I don't tell you something important. But that's what you keep doing."

Daddy stopped looking like there was something funny going on. "You're right," he said.

Suddenly, I was crying. "I don't want to be right." And then I ran into the house. Daddy hates it when I cry. I do too, I hate it when I cry.

I ran to the closet that was all I had after we'd made room for Vicky and Ben and Mack. I slammed the door as hard as I could.

The thing is, usually once I get by myself, I don't feel so much like crying anymore. Sometimes I try to go on crying if I want to make

Mom feel sorry for me. She probably knows that extra crying is fake. She's never said so, but I think she knows.

Daddy knocked on my door. "Go away," I said.

"Lexie, you can't sit in there like Cinderella in the ashes."

Another little flash of anger shot through me. Not as bad as when I'd knocked cookies all over the deck, maybe, but I could easily have spit sparks at Daddy. What I did was open my door and say, "Come back when you know enough not to make jokes."

It was nearly the same thing he says to me when I should apologize for something. *Come back when you know how to behave. Come back when you can sound nicer.* It was just perfect.

And then I shut the door.

Things were pretty quiet out there for the next few seconds. And then there was some whispering. I figured it was Vicky. And maybe Daddy. Probably Daddy.

I wasn't feeling sorry for myself anymore. I waited to see what Daddy would say. And it had better be good.

I opened my book and pretended to read.

Mack opened the door and motored on in. I could see most of the hallway and I couldn't see anybody else out there. I figured Daddy and Vicky had gone back to the table to talk.

Mack didn't look right at me. He had his pink Volkswagen in his hand and he imagined a kind of S-shaped road to the end of my bed and let the Volkswagen putt-putt its way across the sheet to stop at my foot. "Vroom, vrroooom," he said softly. And then he let the motor die out.

"Hi," I said.

He leaned both elbows on my bed and rested there. "Are you coming out?"

"Later," I said.

"I want to dig up the dollar," he said.

"It's too smelly. We can't keep it."

"Can too."

"I guess so." We could lay it in the sun to see if it would dry out like those sand dollars we could buy for a dollar at the marina. And if it didn't, I could buy him one. I had a dollar.

I thought about leaving my room and wondered whether Daddy would think that meant I wasn't mad at him anymore. I wasn't quite as

183

mad at him after getting to say the perfect thing but I thought it might be important to let him think I was. Mom usually had to be mad at Daddy a pretty long time to make him sorry. I wished I had a death look.

"Later," I said to Mack.

"Now," he whispered. And he leaned forward and kissed my big toe. My very dirty big toe.

My heart just melted. "You're a nice boy, do you know that?" That is my most favorite thing my grandmother says to me. Except she doesn't say that I'm a boy.

He nodded. He knew.

"I have to sit here right now. Then I have to call my mom, and after that, I'll go help you dig up the sand dollar."

His motor started right up, but he didn't go anywhere.

"There's a sand pail over there in the corner," I said, pointing to a blue bucket with a green shovel. "It's my very favorite one." It used to be, until it couldn't hold enough stuff. It had been in the storage room for a couple of summers without getting used. "I could meet you on the steps."

Daddy came down the hall and stuck his head in the door. "Can we try again?"

Mack gave me a look that said he knew I was sort of bribing him. He took the bucket and motored to the doorway.

"I want to call Mom," I said to Daddy. "I told her I'd call yesterday."

"Now, look, Lexie . . . ," Daddy said.

I said, "You have to call her first."

"Lexie's right," Vicky said from the hallway.

"I know that," Daddy said. "Weren't we saying that?"

"Of course," Vicky said. She stepped around Daddy to look in. "We're letting Lexie know we agree with her. Mack, why don't we go outside?"

Daddy came in and perched on the end of my bed, bumping his head on the slanted ceiling. "Ow! Guess it's a good thing you're short."

"Only Mack is that short," I said, pulling my knees up so he'd have room to sit.

"I'm sorry I didn't tell you Vicky and I are making plans. I should have made sure you got to know each other sooner."

I wished he'd said that before instead of making that stupid joke.

"I thought we'd tell you here at the beach," Daddy said. "I meant to wait until the end of the week."

"Mom might be sad about you and Vicky," I said.

"I'm a little sad about this too," Daddy said. "I still care when your mom feels bad. I think I know how she'll feel this time. Like the sad part is a whole lot less important than the happy times she has with you and also the man she's dating."

"George."

Daddy was quiet for a minute. Then he said, "I'm sorry. I was so busy hoping you'd like Vicky and the boys, I didn't think about what might be worrying you."

I put my chin on my knees.

"I have a lot of shortcomings," Daddy said, "but not caring about you is not one of them."

"I know," I said.

Daddy laughed. "Thanks, I think. Let's call your mom. Then we can get this vacation back on track, right?"

I had to think about that for a second. Really, I'd been having a pretty good time. It was different than I expected it to be, but it was good all the same. I'd forgotten that for a little while.

Getting up, Daddy bumped his head again. "Ow!"

Twenty-Three

In the kitchen, Vicky was sitting at the table. Mack made a sound like nnyyeer as he ran a tiny red car along the edges. He didn't stop except to zip around Vicky.

"I'm going to make a call," Daddy said over the car sounds.

Vicky looked at me, not smiling her Mary Tyler Moore smile, but a different one, a smaller one that I could believe. "Harris and I can wait out on the deck."

"You don't have to go anywhere," Daddy said, starting to dial.

I had a feeling this was a big moment. But it

was Daddy's big moment. I said, "Mack and I have to go dig up a sand dollar."

Mack came to a sudden stop. His smile was bright, like headlights.

"Do I dare ask *why* you're digging up a sand dollar?" Vicky asked him.

"To keep it," he said. He picked up the sand pail. "Right in here."

"First it has to stay outside for a long time," I told him.

Vicky nodded. "A very long time."

"Hey, it's me," Daddy said into the phone. "She's fine. She's heading out to find something on the beach. Do you have a few minutes to talk?"

Outside, Ben was standing up to his waist in the oncoming waves, braced as if he expected to get knocked over. "Hey, look, Ben's going swimming."

"It's too wet," Mack said.

"Okay, well, we're doing something else anyway."

As Mack and I started down the steps, he grabbed my hand. He was still furry and sandy, only more than before. I tried not to think about it.

"Don't you want to get married?" Mack asked me.

"I think it's okay," I said, because little kids like to get answers right away. And they know what they want to hear.

Once I said it, I thought it was probably true.

We walked along the beach for a little while. I didn't know if we could find that sand dollar again. Mack was puttering along beside me, and he wasn't making motor sounds. Under his breath, he was saying, thoop, thoop, thoop. He made me smile.

"There it is," he said, pointing to a little mound of sand.

We dug down a little bit, and sure enough, there it was, all soft and smelly. "Yuck," Mack said, holding up his green plastic shovel. It had a little piece of sand dollar clinging to it.

"Let's cover it up again," I said. "If Daddy takes us over to the boardwalk, we can buy a very nice one. All dried out."

While we did that, I kept seeing something out of the corner of my eye. Something red stayed at the edge of the water lapping at the sand. I expected it to be a piece of plastic, floating. When I went over and picked it up, Mack drew in a loud breath. It was a shell with claws.

"It's a hermit crab," I said. "The crab lives inside the shell. See where this paint is rubbing off? Somebody must have bought it and set it loose."

"Like the shark."

"Like that."

"Does it bite?"

"You pick it up by the shell." I showed him how. Legs waved in the air. Mack backed up a little and looked it over without touching.

"Can we keep it?" he asked.

"We can." I put it in his bucket.

On the way back I told him about the aquarium with the parsley and the hermit crab pool.

"Is this your hermit crab?" he asked me.

"I think your mom will let you keep it," I said. "What would you name a crab?"

"Volkswagen," he said. "It looks like one."

"Volksy," I said, like *aww*.

"Volkswagen."

Ben was sitting on the deck with Vicky when we got upstairs. His hair was still dry. But he'd gone into the water, that was a good beginning.

Mack rushed over to show them his prize. He picked it up by the shell and held it out. "Eek!" Vicky said, and made him laugh.

"I hope you don't expect us to eat that," Ben said, teasing.

"Nope," Mack said, very serious.

I heard Daddy's voice coming from inside the house. I went to the door, wondering if he was still talking to Mom. When he spoke again, he said, "I guess I thought it would be hard news for you. Lexie made me see how wrong I was to keep waiting for the right moment. As if that could ever come."

That had to mean Mom knew he was going to marry Vicky. It made me feel so much better that I felt sick and dizzy all over again. I could talk to Mom. She'd know why I didn't call.

I walked into the kitchen, Mack motoring along at my side. "We all have to grow up some-time," Daddy said to Mom. He smiled at me. "I'm lucky to get a second chance."

I put out my hand for the phone. "Here, Lexie wants to talk to you," Daddy said.

Mack held the crab up for Daddy to see as I took the phone.

"Very cool," Daddy said, looking impressed.

"You okay?" Mom asked me right away.

"Yep." And I really was. But tears burned in my eyes.

Daddy walked out on the deck, Mack chugging along beside him, the hermit crab's legs waving in the air.

Mom asked, "Does it feel a little weird out there?"

"It's getting better now."

"Really?"

"Really." I figured Mom felt a little weird now. "Is that okay?"

"It is," she said. "We'll have some new friends." And after a moment she added, "You'll have brothers. I just thought of that."

I didn't feel like talking about that yet. "Mom? Are you eating out for breakfast?"

"Every morning."

"Have you seen any movies?"

"Two so far."

I had to think for a moment to know what question I really wanted to ask. And then, when I knew, I asked, "How's that going?"

"Pretty good. Fine, really. We ate spaghetti with meatballs and thought of you."

George says my favorite movie, *Lady and the Tramp,* is his favorite movie. From his childhood. That always makes me laugh, I don't know why.

I took a deep breath. "Are you thinking about marrying George?"

"No, but, Lexie?"

"Yeah?"

"If the thought pops into my head, you'll be the first to know."

"Thanks, Mom."

Mack motored back in with the hermit crab and stood next to me, like he was waiting in line to talk to Mom. The crab waved its tiny claws in the air.

Mom asked, "What's that noise I hear? Is the fridge working okay?"

"The fridge is fine," I said. "That's Mack. Like the truck."

"Mack?"

"We found a hermit crab and Mack is going to take it home," I said. "We might loan him the aquarium."

Mom laughed a little. "You're already acting like a big sister."

Daddy came back inside. "I'm going now. I love you," I said to Mom. I passed Daddy the phone and said, "I love you too."

He tapped the top of his head with his knuckles. *Ol-luv you.*

I watched Mack motor the crab around the shelf with my collection. I didn't worry that he'd touch something. While I wasn't worrying about that, Ben looked inside. "Hey, Mack, you want to go in the water?"

His motor rumbled.

"How about you?" Ben asked me. "You want to go swimming?"

Mack said, "It's too wet."

"Sometimes we have to get wet," Ben said. "I'll go first."

I grinned and said, "I'll go first. And when I come out, my hair will be too wet."

"All right, then," Ben said. "You swim and I'll guard."

"Me too," Mack said.

"Deal," I said, and we went outside to check out the water.

Acknowledgments

With every book I owe a debt of gratitude to people who, in a moment of everyday theater, inspire the story, and children, so honest and courageous, are always an inspiration. Thanks, Susan, for years of reading and commenting on stories in progress, and for letting me share some family moments, and thanks for beach titles as well. And congratulations, you have an agent!

And to people who read and reread and help me make each book the best it can be. And then they put it between knockout covers and put it in the hands of readers everywhere and then, funnily enough, tell me *I* did a good job. Thanks, Shana and company, for all that you do for me. Thanks go to Jill, too, for heading the appreciation committee.

Last on my list, first in my heart, my family. Two kids (the big worrier and the one with furry fingers) and their fine dad, who encouraged me in every way one person meaningfully supports another from the very first page.

About the Author

Audrey Couloumbis's first book for children, *Getting Near to Baby*, won the Newbery Honor in 2000. Audrey is also the author of several other highly acclaimed books for young readers, including *The Misadventures of Maude March* (a Book Sense 76 Pick and a New York Public Library 100 Titles for Reading and Sharing Selection), *War Games* (an NCSS-CBC Notable Social Studies Trade Book for Young People and a *Horn Book* Fanfare Best Book of the Year), which she coauthored with her husband, Akila Couloumbis, and *Jake* (a *Parents' Choice* Recommended Award Winner and a Bulletin Blue Ribbon Book). Audrey lives in upstate New York and Florida with her dog, Phoebe, and Phoebe's two pet parakeets, Tweedle Dee and Tweedle Dum.